DUSTY

Books by THOMAS C. HINKLE:

TAWNY	BARRY
BLACK STORM	HURRICANE PINTO
BUGLE	SHAG
TRUEBOY	CINCHFOOT
SILVER	KING
TORNADO BOY	CRAZY DOG CURLY
BING	BUCKSKIN
OLD NICK AND BOB	DUSTY
SHEP	MUSTANG
TOMAHAWK	JUBE

BLACKJACK

DUSTY

The Story of a Wild Dog

by

THOMAS C. HINKLE

WILDSIDE PRESS

DUSTY

To Elizabeth

Author's Note

========

I have good authority for saying that Old Gray, the she-wolf, might easily have accepted Dusty for her own under the circumstances narrated in the story.

It is interesting in this connection to note that there are several authenticated cases in the old West where dogs crossed with wolves.

T. C. H.

Contents

CONTENTS

DUSTY

I

Old Gray

THE two big black mules walked steadily forward with long swinging strides in the bright starlit night, pulling an old covered wagon behind them. Two men sat on the seat, one of them driving, who now and then spoke to the mules to keep them at a rapid walk. Usually the wagon would have stopped at sunset, but water still was ahead, which made it necessary to travel on into the night some ten miles more to reach the place.

At the rear of the wagon, behind a great pile of boxes, lay a giant mother wolfhound, nursing her nine-day-old puppies—ten of them. The mother dog was content to lie quietly on the hay in spite of the jolting of the wagon, for the puppies had long been whining for their milk and she knew they were very hungry. Ten pups were a large litter, and the fact that one of the puppies was not with the others, for the moment, was not noticed by the mother dog.

It happened that the rocky trail over which the wagon moved caused it to lurch and jolt considerably and one of the pups had been jolted away from the others toward the rear of the wagon. Like the other pups, he was still blind, but he instinctively tried to find his way back to the life-giving milk of his mother. All would soon have been well for him except for an unfortunate accident. Near the rear of the old wagon bed was a broken board, leaving a small opening. A thin covering of hay lay over this opening, concealing it, and the big mother dog was not aware of any possible danger to one of her offspring.

At this moment two things happened. The ground here was thick-set with clumps of low bushes, and the mules were passing over the low brush, pulling the wagon after them. At the same time a hind wheel struck a rock and the wagon lurched so that the lone puppy, near the end-gate, was thrown onto the thin covering of hay over the hole. For a second the hay seemed to hold, but his small body was too heavy for it, and the blind puppy fell through the hole and down through the branches of the thicket to the moist earth below. His weak whining cries were drowned by the loud rasping sounds of the brush scratching against the wagon as it passed over the thicket.

The frail puppy pushed out his weak fore-legs on the moist earth and he moved his head tremblingly from side to side, instinctively hunting for the milk and warmth that would continue his life. Fortunately for him there was no living thing in the thicket here except himself. An owl flew over the place but the thick brush covered the puppy completely and the owl swept on, looking down on the open grassy plain, hunting for any small animal that might be out in the night.

As time went by, the western spring night grew more and more chill and the weak whines of the puppy in the thicket became faint, and fainter still. A brisk wind sprang up which blew through the buck-brush with a whispering, sighing sound, and the swaying, rustling thickets seemed to be the only movement in the lonely starlit night. But soon a moving form appeared a little east of the thicket, stopped suddenly and stood very still. This was a thing of the wild, an old gray she-wolf who had encountered tragedy some twenty-four hours before.

About five miles northwest of this place the old she-wolf, known on the Rolland Horn cattle range as Old Gray, had had a den in a hole on a steep hillside, and in this den were her six young whelps. During the morning hours, while she was away hunting, a wild stampede of longhorn cattle had thundered across the hills and the trembling earth and rocks had given way above the den. When she returned an hour later, she found the den covered with tons of earth and rock, a veritable landslide that entombed her offspring as hopelessly as if they had been a part of the hill itself. Old Gray had stayed at the place and lay for hours in silent misery. But some time, after the night and the stars came, she arose and set forth, she knew not where. And by accident she crossed the trail of the covered wagon.

The reason she stopped quickly here was because she scented the puppy in the thicket, and the faintest of sounds reached her ears. She pointed her nose toward the thicket and sniffed very carefully for any tell-tale scent of an enemy. Assuring herself there was none, she trotted up to the thicket and in great curiosity began to push her way slowly into the buck-brush. She soon reached the weak and now badly chilled puppy.

Probably the old wolf's nose told her that this was the offspring of a dog. And, having had experience with the ranchmen's dogs, she knew them as enemies. But the circumstances here were unusual. For Old Gray, she-wolf though she was, knew that no matter how much she hated the big dogs in general, this weak frail puppy was no enemy to anybody or anything. There was not enough of him to be bad or to hurt anyone. And then there arose in Old Gray something that made her act at once. Somehow, just at this critical time, the frail little puppy seemed like one of her own that she had lost. She gently licked the puppy two or three times, and as any dog mother would have done, she turned around two or three times in the thicket to make room for herself, then lay down and, picking up the puppy gently in her mouth, she pulled him to her warm fur and aching udders.

Instinct caused the puppy—who was destined to be known as Dusty—to follow nature, and so he had the milk he needed. An hour later, when he was fed and warmed, Old Gray picked him up by the nape of the neck and very carefully pushed out of the thicket. She knew now where she was going. When she got out on the open land she took a little firmer hold on the puppy's neck and then trotted and, at times, loped, until she had traveled about three miles up to a rocky ledge high on a hillside. The hill here was thickly covered with trees and brush, and a long thicket shielded the rocky den from sight on the valley below. A thick-set growth of cedars covered much of the hillside down to the valley.

Old Gray gently laid the puppy down before the den and smelled the inside to assure herself that all was safe. She then carried him to the rear of the dark den, where she warmed and fed him until nearly noon of that day. Then while her adopted puppy lay sound asleep in the den, she crawled out to the opening, and with her head outside she looked down on the valley. A small herd of red and white cattle was grazing on the first grass of spring and Old Gray looked hungrily upon them. All at once she raised her head and looked across at the opposite hill. Then she darted into a nearby thicket and pushed through it until only her big head was in the clear. There she lay, and in the cover looked intently at the hillside opposite. Two big timber wolves had suddenly appeared there. They were both black in color, a male and female.

Old Gray knew they had long been her enemies. Her mate had disappeared two weeks before, and since he and she had had several clashes with these two black wolves on this particular range, she had an instinctive feeling that they had something to do with her mate's disappearance. Her mate had not been a large wolf and so would have been unequal to the two black wolves on the opposite hill. But Old Gray was big. She weighed much more than a hundred pounds, probably around one hundred and forty, and she could fight like a tiger. She knew the two big wolves were getting ready to attack the cattle below and she waited, for she was now very hungry.

The two black wolves kept under cover of the trees and brush on the hill and so worked

their way down until they were on the edge
of the valley. Suddenly the two wolves
rushed swiftly and fell upon a cow before
the herd was aware of them. Away ran the
cattle, but the victim went down and the two
big wolves fell to the feed. As they ate together, suddenly they were startled. Old
Gray had appeared nearby and, with deadly
snarls and greenish, gleaming eyes, she ad-
vanced toward them. The sheer ferocity in
her made the black beasts give way a little.
As Old Gray fed on the back of the carcass,
the two wolves moved toward the front end
of the beef and there tore at the feed, all the
while watching her. After a time all the
wolves raised their heads and looked toward
the hills on the east. Instantly they all ran
away. The two black wolves ran up the hill
under cover of the trees and thickets and so
over the hill and away.

Old Gray ran with all her might toward

her den and reached it before the cause of
the alarm made their appearance. Crouching
near her den Old Gray saw two horsemen
ride over the hill on this side and on down to
the valley. The wolves had not seen the men
but they had gotten the strong scent of them.
She watched the men intently as they rode
down the hillside and up to the freshly killed
cow. When they dismounted and began to
move about the carcass Old Gray knew from
experience that they were doing something
that made the carcass deadly dangerous to her
for food. And she was right.

The two riders were Rolland Horn, the
owner of the vast Horn ranch, and a fifteen-
year-old youth, Matt Henderson, whom Rolland Horn had cared for since Matt was a
little boy. Rolland's favorite name for Matt
was Son.

Rolland and Matt carried poison for the
purpose of killing off the wolves that at-

tacked the cattle, and they were now cutting slits in the meat and dropping in little pellets of strychnine. They went on with their work for some time, putting poison in the carcass, not knowing that Old Gray lay behind the cover of the low thicket up the hill, watching them. The tall ranch owner and the slim youth finally mounted their horses and rode away. When they were a quarter of a mile down the valley, Old Gray pushed a little farther out of the brush where she could get a better view of them. If it had not been for Dusty back in the dark den she would not have cared much in which direction the two humans went, but now, with this small helpless thing to take care of, Old Gray watched the two riders until they rode out of sight around a spur of the hill. Then she got to her feet and walked out on the open hillside. She could see nothing below but the carcass of the cow near the small stream and a lone cedar.

She moved watchfully down the hill and up to the carcass. She walked around it twice, sniffing at the meat. After this she walked behind a thicket near the small stream that flowed through the valley, and there she sat where she could look down the valley in the direction Matt Henderson and Rolland Horn had taken. The wind blew steadily and it stirred the long gray hair on her side and neck while it whispered and rustled through the branches of the thicket. At the margin of the nearby stream a small drift had caught on some willow roots and there came the steady low murmuring of the water around the little drift. Everything remained undisturbed, as nature had made it, around here and down the valley at the spur of the hill. Old Gray turned to look with concern at the hillside across the valley where the two black wolves had disappeared. She saw nothing there but the clumps of cedar trees and brushy thickets standing on the hill. There was no sign of life except two crows that kept flying restlessly about in the top of a tall cottonwood in the valley near the river.

Old Gray walked up the hillside to the thicket in front of her den, turned and looked searchingly over the valley and at the opposite hill, then made her way around the thicket and up to the den from behind the bushes. She went in and found Dusty hungry. Old Gray lay there, her head up and her eyes shining, facing the opening of the den where she could see a faint light.

During these first days Dusty knew nothing except that he was comfortable. In due time his eyes came open, but day after day he lay in the darkness of the den, spending much of his time sleeping. As the days went by he awakened each time Old Gray darkened the opening of the den as she came in.

Dusty was four weeks old before Old Gray

took him outside the den into the sunlight. It was a new and delightful experience to him, lying on a small bed of soft warm earth with the life-giving sunlight streaming upon him. He lay here an hour sleeping while Old Gray watched all around the place. He might have gone on sleeping there another hour, but suddenly he felt the quick pressure of Old Gray's teeth on his neck and she hustled him into the dark den. Two riders had appeared on the hilltop above so suddenly that Old Gray was fortunate in dodging into the den unseen.

She was more concerned than she used to be about something like this. She was troubled because she had not heard the horses sooner, and while Old Gray did not exactly know that age had now dulled her hearing, she did know that something was wrong with her and she was troubled as she lay in the den with Dusty, who was again asleep against her warm fur. She wanted to protect him with everything in her power and, while she lay there looking at the faint light of the den opening, a new sense of caution came to her. Since she had been so completely surprised by the men she would not take such a chance again for a long time. She knew by instinct that Dusty needed sunlight, but if by giving him this the men might find him, it would be better for him to stay in the den.

One morning when Dusty was six weeks old he awakened to find himself alone in the den. He could see the light coming in faintly from the opening and he was very curious. Slowly he walked toward the streak of light and when he was within a few feet of the opening he stopped and stood for some time blinking. Something urged him irresistibly and he slowly walked outside where he was at first almost blinded by the light. He moved in under the overhanging green thicket near the den and after a time he quit blinking his eyes, for now he could see. Everything around was strange to him but he was not afraid. He did not know the difference between Old Gray who had mothered him and the big wolfhound who was his own mother and had cared for him his first days. But Dusty had of late begun to have strange feeling when Old Gray came in and uttered sounds to him that he did not understand. Already he was more like a wild thing than if he had been raised by his own mother, yet he was a dog, not a born wolf, and it was hard to understand this wolf training.

All at once Dusty was startled. Old Gray seemed to come from nowhere and the first thing Dusty knew she had nipped him sharply. Acting on a natural impulse, he yelped and ran into the den where he crowded back in the farthest dark corner. Old Gray came in and lay down beside him, uttering low growls and licking her great fangs. Dusty presently forgot about the nip she had given him and after getting his milk he again went to sleep, with his small body resting against the heavy fur of Old Gray.

A week later Dusty awakened and again found himself alone. He did not know why he was so much alone these days. He did not know that since Old Gray had lost her mate she had to hunt food for herself and Dusty. All that Dusty knew was that if no one was looking he would get outside the den in the warm sunlight. When he got to the mouth of the den he poked his head outside and again he looked about the place. He could see better on this day. Just in front of the den was a space where there was a spot of soft warm earth that Old Gray had dug up purposely for him to lie on when she chose to bring him outside. Dusty lay down here and looked sharply on both sides of him. He remem-

bered the nip Old Gray had given him before
and he was afraid she might come up quickly
and do that again, but on this day he suc-
ceeded in his venture.

He remained outside nearly two hours before he went back in the dark den. Soon Old
Gray came in and she licked him a few times
while she got him close to her.

When he was two months old, Old Gray
began to bring small game to him. Once she
brought a dead rabbit; again she came in
with a dead ground squirrel. And so Dusty
learned to eat meat. Old Gray now allowed
him to come out of the den and she would lie
a little distance away where she could watch
while Dusty ate of some small game she had
brought in.

During these days Old Gray tried to teach
Dusty as she had taught so many of her offspring, but from the beginning she had a lot

of trouble with this little creature she had found in the buck-brush.

Late one afternoon she took him outside where she lay down on some soft earth close to the den. Little streaks of sunlight came through the thicket and fell on Dusty and he was very comfortable. He began to roll over on his back and stretch his legs while his eyes smiled at things in general. Old Gray watched him with wild greenish eyes and she often turned her head to look out on the hillside and also up and down the valley. She lay here for some time watching Dusty entertain himself, when suddenly not far down the valley she saw a lone horseman galloping along the river. Instantly she uttered the wolf warning sound and dived into the den, but to her amazement Dusty did not follow her as a wolf pup would have done. She came out quickly and gave Dusty such a nip that he ran into the den, not because he was afraid of the horseman, but of this strange mother. Once inside the den with her, she began licking him gently and he forgot everything except that he wanted more milk. He was big enough now to be weaned but Old Gray let him alone.

As time went by and Dusty was allowed to go out of the den more and more, he learned by being nipped so often that when Old Gray made a certain sound, she would nip him again if he did not dive in the den at once. But he did not have the fear of men she wanted him to have. This she discovered one day when she crouched low and hid in some brush and watched two riders gallop past her and along the hillside where they were looking for some calves. When Old Gray reached the den she saw, to her great fear, Dusty not only outside the den but standing on a hump of earth above it and calmly looking at the two cowboys riding down the valley.

If one of them had chanced to look up the hill he certainly could have seen Dusty standing there. His color itself was striking enough, for Dusty had a number of white spots on each side. And his ears did not stand erect like those of the gray wolf but lopped down like the Irish wolfhound.

Old Gray was badly frightened for Dusty. She uttered a quick warning sound and it was Dusty's turn to be afraid because he remembered that sound meant "hide quick." He ran to the den and dived in. He rushed to the rearmost part of the den and there he lay, his heart thumping. He was afraid only of Old Gray. To him everything in the world seemed right and he could no more understand Old Gray than she could understand him. He did not know how much he meant to her, but he did know fully that he must depend on her. If he had been a wolf cub she would have nipped him again, but she was beginning to understand that he was different. She came up affectionately to Dusty and licked him on the head for a time while she lay down very close to him, and all of this was so agreeable to Dusty that he went sound asleep.

All through this night Old Gray was restless. She was deeply concerned for this strange son she had adopted. To her he was not like any of her own wolf whelps, but she nevertheless had a strange affection for him. And because of this she must now begin to train him to shift for himself in the wild range country. She had wanted to begin his training before, but he had troubled her in not doing what she told him. But now that Dusty was getting older his training must begin and it would be a time of danger for him.

Three times, while Dusty lay asleep in the den, Old Gray went outside and sat on the hillside. When she went out there was a

steady wind blowing from the west and the
stars were shining. Small clouds moved restlessly across the sky. No matter how intently
Old Gray looked she saw nothing but the
silent hills and the shadowy valley below the
trees standing like dark sentinels in the star-
light.

Old Gray sat on the hill, looking around
her watchfully, and now and then pointing
her nose in the wind and sniffing carefully
for the scent of enemies. As she sat here the
dawn came, and when the sun itself peeped
up from the east she went into the den and
awakened Dusty. He yawned comfortably
and began to wag his tail and grin at her in
his own way. She gave him his breakfast, and
after one or two affectionate licks with her
tongue she said to him by the sound she
made, "Come! I want you to go with me."

When Dusty came outside of the den behind her she nosed him and tried to get him

to understand that she wanted him to follow
her. He hesitated at first but when she stood
off a little and made the sounds again he came
up to her. When she started down the hill he
was all at once delighted. He pushed through
the tall grass and over the stony places, keeping always very close to her, until they came
to the stream in the valley. Here Old Gray
stood along the edge of the shallow stream
and lapped the water. Dusty walked in the
water until it reached his knees and he, too,
lapped the water. He felt a wild thrill out
here in the sunlight. This was the finest experience he had ever known. And when Old
Gray started down along the margin of the
stream, walking on the wet sand, Dusty
trotted along beside her. As she walked along
the wet sand Old Gray did not know that she
and Dusty were leaving telltale tracks for
certain sharp human eyes. Tracks of the big
gray wolves were frequently seen by the

rangemen, but it was unusual to see the footprints of the young wolves. The tracks of the
young were seen only occasionally.

Old Gray walked along rapidly, with
Dusty trotting beside her, using her nose and
eyes constantly to discover enemies. So that
Dusty might learn how to move in the rough
places, now and then she went away from the
river's edge and walked through tall grass.
At times she crowded through small thickets,
while Dusty, delighted with it all, pushed
along beside her.

Old Gray wanted to train Dusty as she
would if he had been her own, but something
about him seemed wrong. He did not respond
to her every sound with the lightning quickness that a young wolf would have done, but
she would have to take him out often and
train him. And she desired to teach Dusty
what to her was the greatest danger on the
range—men on horses!

After a considerable distance had been covered Old Gray decided this was enough for the time, and going down on the open sand near the river, she started at a rapid trot back to the den.

II

The Wild Dog Pup

IT was in the afternoon of the day when Dusty and Old Gray walked along the river that Matt Henderson galloped around a spur of hill and up the Willow Valley. When he reached the open sandy margin of the stream his horse slowed down to a walk. Suddenly Matt pulled his horse to a stand and dismounted. He looked intently at some tracks he saw in the wet sand. He said under his breath, "A she-wolf and one of her young! But there are generally several young wolf pups. Wonder where the others are?" Slowly

Matt walked along beside the river, looking intently at the tracks in the sand. Farther on he noted that the tracks disappeared in the grass and thickets among the cottonwoods and willows on this side. Matt tied his horse and made his way carefully forward in the woods until he could see out through them and up the hill. He stood for some time looking at every bush and rock and, in particular, he scanned the long rocky ledge running along near the upper part of the hill. He knew that a she-wolf sometimes had her den under such rocky ledges and the trail he had followed turned off in this direction.

Matt was aware that if a she-wolf had a den up there under the ledge she might be in the den with her young, or at this time of day she might be out hunting. In these wild places gray wolves hunted when hungry, day or night. Matt stood long and silently leaning against a tree, looking around it and up

the hillside. He knew that if he wished to see
any life along the high rocky ledge stillness
on his part was necessary. What he hoped was
that if the she-wolf who had made the tracks
was in the den, she would come outside with
her young to sun themselves. He knew this
might happen unless she had already seen
him or his horse.

In the deep stillness a low wind blew down
the hill and started all the cottonwood leaves
to murmuring. Matt looked intently all along
the hillside and it seemed to him that he let
no point escape him along the rocky ledge
above. Then, suddenly, he saw something
that startled him and at the same time made
him feel chagrined. All the time he had been
looking up the hill there had been a dusty-
colored animal in plain sight, sound asleep on
a mound of earth on one side of the rocky
ledge. The animal now awakened, sat up,
yawned and looked down on the valley. And

such an animal out here in this wild valley! It was, Matt knew, either a dog pup or a wolf pup. But it couldn't be a wolf! Not like that! Matt was certain it was a dog. Then as Dusty stood up on all four feet Matt saw the white spots on his sides and the dusty color of the rest of his coat. And the ears did not stand erect like the timber wolf; they lopped down like the big staghounds that Matt had seen many times. Dusty sat down again, yawning, and again looked down on the valley. He raised his ears as much as he could, the way grown staghounds do when they are alert and looking at something. Then Dusty got up and began walking about and sniffing in the short grass.

Certainly, Matt thought to himself, that was surely a dog up there. But how did a pup happen to be out here in this wild place, a pup evidently both well nourished and wholly contented! Was there a wild mother dog out here? It would seem impossible that a mother wolf had in some way taken a dog pup to raise. Then Matt suddenly remembered stories about this. He had heard the men of the West tell of instances where it was positively known that a dog pup had been mothered by a she-wolf. There was the case over on the Twin Bar Ranch where the cowboys shot an old timber wolf while a dog four months old was running with her. The cowboys said the dog was *all* dog, being yellow and white-spotted, with the drooping ears of many domestic dogs. The pup was captured and tamed. Then there was the case over in the Grizzly Canyon region where an animal had been caught in a trap, and by common consent of all who saw it, it was undoubtedly a cross between a timber wolf and a shaggy-haired wolfhound. All this proved to the rangemen that dogs and wolves might, on rare occasions, accompany each other.

Naturally, all these tales and others came to Matt as he stood looking at what he knew for certain was a dog. He hardly dared to move, being afraid that the mother, whatever she was—dog or wolf—might be watching close by.

Slowly Matt edged behind the tree and looked back at his horse. The animal was very tired from the long ride and stood with his head down, his eyes closed, and resting. There was no sound except the steady whispering of the innumerable cottonwood leaves. Matt waited and watched intently for he realized that the wind was in his favor and that he might yet see what it was that had taken such good care of a dog pup in this wild place. It seemed to him that a long time had passed when he saw a movement in a thicket on the hillside well to the south of where he stood, and he knew the movement of the thicket was not caused by the wind.

Then he saw, not a dog, but a big grayish she-wolf, holding a dead rabbit in her mouth. She trotted along the hillside and, to Matt's surprise, he saw the dog pup run to meet her. When she got near the den she dropped the rabbit before the pup and lay down to watch him.

Old Gray no longer objected when she found Dusty out on the mound of earth above the den. He was large and growing quickly and she knew the time was fast coming when he would have to take care of himself in these wild places. She had hunted for him and up to the present she had taken all the chances for him, but while she lay watching him something came over her, something that made her feel that he must now begin to make journeys more often from the den.

After Dusty had finished his meal Old Gray got up from where she lay and made a sound to him that he only half understood.

She started away and he followed her, but suddenly he stopped and sat down, uncertain. This troubled her. She came back to him, put her nose on him, licked him once on the nose with her tongue and, again making the low sound, she started away. Dusty got up and followed her, and after several false starts he got it in his head that he should follow her on indefinitely. He was all at once very happy about this new adventure. He started to run ahead of her down through the thickets on the slope, but she leaped forward and nipped him sharply which brought him back alongside and there he moved forward with her and kept so close he touched her almost constantly.

Matt was so thrilled with the sight before him that he forgot to do more than look. For the first time he thought of his rifle on the saddle. But seeing Dusty made him forget this, and he forgot everything except the strange sight of a pup being mothered by an old she-wolf. The old she-wolf turned a little in her course down the hill and toward the slow-moving stream in the valley. Matt saw what a striking contrast Dusty's color made with the deep green grass when he paused for a moment in an open space.

All at once Old Gray stopped under the shade of a tree and turned her head away from Matt to look down the valley. At the same time Dusty, taking advantage of her stop, trotted off on the green grass, and, as it happened, toward the tree where Matt stood. Matt's mind was in a whirl. He had nothing to catch the big pup with except his hands, and if he ran for his horse, where he had both lariat rope and rifle, perhaps both the pup and the old she-wolf would escape. Even if he had had the rifle he knew that for the first time in his life he would have let a full-grown wolf go on her way in peace! The circumstances here were so very unusual. Certainly there was a real dog pup, and such a pup! And there was a big gray she-wolf— one that Matt now recognized as Old Gray— but she was mothering the pup and it was very plain that without her the pup would not live long—not out here with dangers on every hand.

Not knowing what to do, Matt did nothing but look. He saw the old wolf move along with all the stealth of her kind and at the same time he saw how the pup bothered her by his queer ways of stopping and trying to look at everything. He was evidently not much afraid, whereas a young timber wolf of his age would by this time have been so trained by his mother that he would have been as wild as the young bobcats in the hollow trees of the deep gorges. Matt was sure, however, that if he showed himself the pup would run like a deer.

Suddenly Matt was startled when his horse blew loudly through its nose. At the sound the old she-wolf whirled and darted into some bushes, but Dusty, being a dog and not a wolf, merely looked with curiosity in the direction of the sound. At this the wolf sprang back, nipped him and drove him into the bushes ahead of her, where they both disappeared from sight. Matt watched intently. He saw the tops of the thickets move a little in places along the hillside and he knew the old she-wolf with the dog pup was moving quickly down the valley. He watched, hoping he might see them go into a den. He was about to quit looking and go to his horse when he was startled by sounds down the river. Bang! Bang! Bang! Three shots in rapid succession.

Matt got to his horse, leaped on him and rode hard down the valley. Suddenly he saw two riders plunge out of the river woods and,

on reaching the hill, start up the slope. Matt
shouted and they turned and waited. He
found Rolland Horn and Charley Stone.
Rolland said, "I saw Old Gray and tried to
bring her down, but just after the shots I saw
a dog pup with her—a sure enough dog pup,
dusty-colored and white. Charley and I
wouldn't shoot after that and there wasn't
much time either, for Old Gray and that pup
ran into a den up there in the rocks. I reckon
I missed Old Gray completely and, seeing she
had a dog pup, I hope I didn't hurt her on
account I'm plumb curious about her and that
pup."

Matt told them what he had seen. Rolland
said, "Now think of that—her with a dog
pup. She shot in among these rocks up here
with that same spotted pup. We'll see where
they went in."

"And here it is!" said Matt, who reached
the place first. "Look at their tracks! It's so,

Rolland. Maybe we can trap the pup. The trap won't break his legs if we wrap the trap with rags same as Charley here caught a young timber wolf over on the Bear Canyon Range."

"It's so," said Charley, "and I got a couple of traps on my saddle. I took 'em up from the lower valley this morning. We can set the traps close to the opening here and while Old Gray will know what they are, the pup won't and he may get caught."

"Good," said Rolland. "Now, Charley, set these traps same as you did when you caught the young timber wolf."

Charley cut his stakes and with a big rock these were driven into the earth. Then the traps were carefully wrapped with the bandana handkerchiefs of Rolland, Charley and Matt. When all was done Charley said,

"Now, of course, Old Gray will try to get that pup away from here when she comes out and sees the traps, but I figure that by setting these two traps close maybe he'll get in one of them in spite of Old Gray. I figger that spotted pup may step plumb on a pan of the traps and there he'll holler and all that Old Gray can do will be just to stay by him, for smart as she is she can't get him out. I don't reckon we'll get him by these traps on account of Old Gray, but he *might* step in a trap before she could get him away. And one thing is certain, one of us must be here pretty early in the morning on account if that wild pup *is* caught, and something happened to Old Gray at the same time, why, that pup wouldn't last no time—especially if some of the other timber wolves happened along."

Matt said quickly, "I'll be here early in the morning."

Rolland grinned and said, "I knowed you would, Son. And daggone if I don't get up and come too."

"Me too," said Charley. "I wouldn't want nothing to happen to that pup, except that he gets caught in a trap and we get him."

When the traps were set, Rolland got down and looked in the den. After a minute he said, "I can see two pairs of shining eyes in there. I reckon I could finish Old Gray in there pretty quick. This likely ain't her regular den. She just run in here to save that pup. Well, even if she has helped eat some of the cows I wouldn't be so mean as to take advantage of her with that pup in there— her having no chance at all."

"Sure," said Charley, "and him a plumb purty pup she's caring for."

The place where Dusty and Old Gray were hiding was much like her regular den, except that there was a wide space in front with barren ground and only scant vegetation.

The two traps were set close to the opening of the den. The hope was that Dusty might step into one of them before Old Gray could get him away from the place. Matt, Rolland and Charley did not know how Old Gray ever came by the pup, but they knew timber wolves, and they knew Old Gray would make an effort to get Dusty away from this dangerous place some time in the night.

III

The New Den

OLD GRAY had not got off as easily as Rolland Horn supposed when he and Charley Stone had fired at her down the valley. Rolland's last shot had made a wound in her shoulder and while it was not dangerous it annoyed her as she lay in the dark rocky den with Dusty. Fortunately for her she could reach the wound with her tongue and so keep down some of the discomfort, but to Old Gray this wound was a small matter. She had been slightly wounded in this way a number of times in the wild range country, but she had never had so close a call while she was with her own pups. And somehow it seemed Dusty increased her difficulties. Ever since she started out with him he was a care because he seemed to her to be so stupid about the men. Long before Dusty had any business to do so, it seemed to her, he had come out of the old den and lay on the mound of earth above in the warm sun. She had finally quit bothering him about this. But it seemed strange to her that in spite of the fact that he was outside, he was always safe when she got to the den.

As Old Gray lay in the darkness of the den here she paid less attention to her wound than to Dusty. She spent most of her time looking intently toward the opening and then licking Dusty's head and smoothing his hair. While his actions were strange to her she cared for him in an unusual way—cared enough to fight to the last for him, if that became necessary.

After the manner and patience of wild things Old Gray did not move toward the opening of the den until long after the night had come. When she put her nose out of the opening the moon and stars were shining and the wind was blowing up from the river. Even before she got to the opening of the den she got a smell she knew and detested. It was the smell of iron-jawed traps. When she was a year old she had left a toe of her front foot in one of these things. As she came forward now to the mouth of the den Dusty came close behind her, but she was very careful to see that he did not get out ahead of her. When she was at the mouth of the den she began to be troubled. The men had cunningly set one of the traps so that she could not possibly get out of the den unless she stepped in one of the traps or over and so across it. If she had been alone she could have managed this, but she had Dusty with her. She allowed him to come up until his head was close to hers, then she made a sound that somehow he understood. "Stop! Danger here!" Dusty lay close beside her and looked out on the space in front of the den. He turned his head now to one side and now to the other, then looked up at Old Gray inquiringly as if to say, "What is it? I can't see a thing that looks wrong."

Old Gray lay here for many minutes. She knew that in time it would be dawn and she had long ago learned that the daylight is the time when riders were abroad and the time when she could be easily seen. She also knew that the men had discovered her and Dusty here, and she not only wanted to get him out of this den but wanted to get him as far away as possible in the hope that the men could not follow and so would not know where she had taken him.

Now the cunning of Old Gray began to be manifest. She turned to Dusty and licked him tenderly on the head; then she surprised him by taking a firm hold in the middle of his back as she pushed out of the den. Dusty was heavy now but Old Gray was strong and powerful.

Of necessity Old Gray gripped hard and this hurt Dusty who whined in protest. But Old Gray moved forward, and as she slid out of the den her forequarters slid upward so that Dusty's hind legs and all were safely above the dangerous trap jaws. Now came what the cowboys would have called the ticklish part of it. Old Gray, slowly, very slowly, moved one long front leg forward and over the nearest trap, then she moved the other front leg. This done, she paused for a second, her front legs on one side of the trap and her hind legs on the other. Suddenly gathering her powerful muscles, she lurched forward and brought her hind legs over the trap. The trap on the other side of this one was easily avoided.

She carried Dusty halfway down the slope before she let him go. She stopped only long enough to lick him a little with her tongue and tell him how glad she was he was safe. He whimpered a little and looked up at her, but when she hurried down the slope he ran close beside her until they reached the river. There she licked him again on his head, as if she were saying, "My! That was an awful thing we escaped from! Come! Let us drink a little here and then I'm going to find a place where I can hide you so none of those two-legged animals will know. You don't know as yet and you don't seem to learn about such creatures very fast, but in time you'll wake up! So come along now. We'll drink here and then we must find a place where I can hide you before the daylight comes." Old Gray drank and Dusty drank, also, but he was not very thirsty. Then Old Gray, for some reason known to her, decided to cross the narrow stream. She waded in a little way but Dusty hesitated to follow.

As on so many other occasions, she was bothered because he seemed so much slower in learning than her own wolf pups. But she was equal to the occasion. She picked him up by the nape of the neck and carried him out into the stream where the water was up to her middle. There she let Dusty down and she herself plunged on below her depth. Dusty swam easily beside her, his head out of the water, and he made no sound except to grunt a little now and then, as if the effort was almost comfortable to him. They had to swim only a short distance before they came to the shallows where the stream flowed over the sandy bottom. Old Gray splashed out of the stream on the other side where there was no woods. She and Dusty shook themselves vigorously while standing on the green grass above the water. Then Old Gray hurried down the river with Dusty loping clumsily after her. When the dawn came she turned into a wild hillside where great masses of rocks lay about in profusion. Here and there tall cedars stood in the silence as if watching the approach of these two strange companions, an old she-wolf and a dusty and white pup. On and up the wild slope Old Gray led Dusty. Once he stopped to smell the strange scents under a cedar and once he began to smell the ground near a big boulder, but each time Old Gray came back, put her nose close to him and made sounds that he now understood fairly well. She was saying to him, "Don't stop to look. Come! Danger may be near!"

Old Gray led Dusty up the hill until she reached a point far up the slope. Here, directly before her, was a high, sheer, rocky wall that extended a long distance along the hill. Old Gray cast one look up the sheer face of the cliff, then she looked quickly to the right and left. She turned and looked down on the valley. The place where she stood was of solid rock and there were a number of dark dens at the base of the high rocky steep. While Old Gray stood looking down on the valley Dusty sat close beside her, but he could see nothing that interested him. Finally he got to his feet and put his nose up as high as he could toward Old Gray's head. She did not seem to notice him. She was looking and, at the same time, sniffing the wind for scents of her most dangerous enemies—the black wolves and the men.

Presently Old Gray turned and began to hunt for a den here. She smelled in several, then decided. She put her nose to Dusty's and said in the language he now knew, "This one will do. Follow me."

Old Gray crouched down and made her way inside, with Dusty crowding in so close he touched her. He was old enough now so that he would have been afraid to go in there unless Old Gray had led the way. He accepted her as if she had been his mother in every way, even though some of her ways were strange to him. And there was one thing that was growing on him—a certain devotion to her. He was getting old enough to understand his need of her in all this strange uncertain world.

Old Gray spent a little time in this den of almost solid rock, moving about to every corner of it. Dusty moved around in the darkness behind her and tried to investigate in his own way, smelling at the places she did. After a time she made her way outside the den and Dusty was right beside her. Old Gray lay down and looked into the valley—and she looked with deep anxiety. She knew that this den was safe enough to keep Dusty from danger in time of stress, yet she knew he could not stay in the den always. Her instinct made her know that he must grow and develop, and live among the dangers of the wild places where she had grown up and lived and faced the scars of battle and constant danger. As Old Gray looked down on the valley this time she thought of the two savage, black, killer wolves. She knew the danger to Dusty from those creatures if he was ever caught out too far from the rocky den.

The day passed with no danger to Dusty or herself. When the night fell she took Dusty into the den. He felt very sleepy and soon went sound asleep where he lay. Old Gray put her nose close to him with deep concern. She must go out now and hunt food. Would he stay here in the dark den where she had brought him? This thought troubled her, but they must eat, and while he slept she stole out and quietly slipped away in the night. She must not be gone long. Not with this queer foster son in the den. He was so wonderful to have but also he was queer and strange. Danger lurked everywhere in this wild region, yet he did not seem to know. She felt that she must hurry with the hunting and get back to the den with food for him. Old Gray was fortunate, returning in about an hour with a rabbit which she and Dusty ate together.

The especial danger to Old Gray and Dusty at this time were the two black wolves already mentioned. They were a big black male and female, each weighing well over one hundred pounds. Both were larger than the average timber wolf and both were savage to an extreme degree. The black female seemed to have instilled some of her own ferocity into the big male and they roamed the range to drive out or destroy all creatures whatever.

The timber wolf of ordinary size was no match for them, but Old Gray was a giant wolf herself, although she was past her prime. And while the two black wolves might overcome her if they attacked together, still the two black marauders knew there was danger to them also. They did not know that Old Gray was really getting old and already her once lance-like fangs were becoming dulled from long use. Old Gray, however, had the fire of battle in her and now that she had Dusty to care for she was more watchful than ever.

The next morning Old Gray went outside the den and sat down. Dusty came out with her and began playfully to gnaw at her long

rough hair, growling low as he did so. Old
Gray kept looking intently down in the valley and now and then she turned her head to
look quickly on either side of her. She acted
as if she were paying no attention to Dusty
as he wooled and tugged at the hair on her
neck, but the truth was she was very proud
of him. She looked at him, now, with a soft
light in her eyes. She liked to hear him growl
and she also liked to feel his small teeth, for
she knew that if he were to live in these dangerous places he would need sharp teeth and
he would have to watch and be ready for battle at any time. As Old Gray watched and
sniffed the air she knew that, while this place
here was a good one for her and Dusty to
hide in, it was possible for the two wolves to
approach from behind the giant boulders and
cedars along the hillside. Old Gray felt secure for the moment, but she could not see
everything. While she lay here, and Dusty

playfully chewed at the hair on her neck, something she could not see was happening down the river in a deep woods at that point.

The two black wolves were moving through the woods in a bend down the river. They came out near the stream under some low-hanging willows where their forms could not have been seen even though one had been looking in their direction. They came forward, the savage female leading, and for a few seconds both stood side by side, heads lowered, looking at the woods on the other side. Suddenly the female quickly raised her head and sniffed the low breezes blowing across the river and stirring in the leaves in the nearby willows. The wind blew from Old Gray and Dusty toward these enemies. The big male wolf also looked up and sniffed the air and by a common impulse both wolves got back under deeper cover of the willows, where they stood watching for a few seconds. Assuring themselves the game was some distance up the river, they came from under the willows and quickly passed down to the stream where they plunged in and, getting beyond their depth, began to swim across, only their black heads showing above the water. When they reached the other side they ran forward in the cover of the trees until they came to a point where the woods ended, and here under cover of a deep thicket they sniffed the air and looked up the boulder-studded hillside. Suddenly they saw Old Gray and Dusty.

Old Gray sat not far from the den. Dusty rolled over on his back, and with eyes laughing he bit playfully at the stones around him, at times wriggling around and acting as if he wanted to bite something out of reach. An hour went by as Old Gray remained outside the den to watch for enemies. She saw no riders anywhere in the valley below and not even a tell-tale breeze brought to her the scent of the two black enemies hiding in the woods below. These two beasts continued to hide in the thicket and to look not so much at Old Gray as at Dusty. To them he was a young dog and of all creatures these marauders of the range detested dogs since they were the companions of men.

But at this time the two wolves were wary of Old Gray. They could not understand why she would take in a dog pup as she had, but because the pup was at the moment playing and tugging at her neck they knew it was so. They knew what would happen if they should attack at this time. Old Gray would fight them like a tigress. Even though they were together they hesitated, but the female licked her jaws while she looked at the queer scene above where the spotted pup played around Old Gray.

The wind still remained in the wrong di-

rection for Old Gray to scent the two wolves,
but she had her eyes and she turned her head
in every direction to watch for enemies.
Then the two black wolves decided to come a
little closer. Believing they would not be
seen, they moved swiftly to the shelter of a
big gray boulder a little out from the woods
on the hillside. Quick as they were, however,
Old Gray saw the sudden movement, and
even as they darted behind the boulder she
saw and recognized her enemies. She had got
no scent, however, and only the briefest look,
but that look was enough. She astonished
Dusty by pinching him suddenly with her
great fangs and he rushed into the den ahead
of her. She crawled in after him into the
dark place where she lay still.

Dusty did not know what had happened
and in a little time began to wool at Old
Gray, for he had not finished his play. But
Old Gray set her wild eyes on the dim light

that came in the den. She was not afraid of attack in the den and she felt Dusty was safe there. But she was disturbed because she believed her two enemies had seen her young one. Old Gray was not afraid of both the black wolves together. She had only contempt for them. But Dusty complicated matters for her very much.

In the meantime the two wolves saw they had been discovered. They dashed back in the woods and watched from that cover. They had seen both Old Gray and her strange young one go into the den far up the hillside among the rocks.

Suddenly the two wolves rushed for the deeper cover of the woods. Coming up the valley near the river was a lone rider. And for the time they forgot Old Gray and her strange pup while they hurried away to a deep rocky gorge not far to the east where their den was hidden by a thick growth of low thickets high up the side of a gorge.

Old Gray had not seen the rider who, at the moment, was hidden from her sight by a fringe of timber along the river. And now that she had got Dusty in the den she felt he was secure from the two wolves. As for herself she would hunt where she pleased. She was big and powerful still, and no wolf ever lived that she greatly feared. It was true she knew there was some danger to her if both the black wolves attacked her. In due time she would take Dusty out and teach him how he, too, must hunt to live, but she postponed doing it because she dreaded it on his account. She would do all the hunting for a time. And there was much of it to do for Dusty was nearly always hungry. He was hungry at this moment. She knew for he had stopped his play and made low whining sounds that told her the hunger in him was again calling for meat.

Old Gray crawled out of the den. Dusty followed her. She turned and made a sound that caused him to scramble back into the den, but he didn't go far back—just enough so he wouldn't be noticed. There he lay and watched the big form of Old Gray where she remained a short time, looking on all sides. She still did not see the lone horseman and so felt free to hunt as she pleased. Looking back toward the den to make sure Dusty would not follow, she unfortunately started toward the hidden rider.

Old Gray did not see the lone rider because he had dismounted from his horse and was looking at some wolf tracks behind a screen of willows. This rider, Abe Rivers, was a cowboy strange to the region, and was on his way to the Rolland Horn ranch, hunting work. It happened he had taken his rifle from the saddle. Suddenly he saw an old female wolf running away from him. He fired and saw the wolf fall. Thinking he had gotten his game he mounted his horse and galloped in that direction, but to his surprise and disgust the wolf leaped up and disappeared in the deep woods before he could again get his rifle ready. Abe hunted about in the woods until near sunset and when he got to the Rolland Horn ranch house it was late. When he related his story, he was astonished at the effect on all the other riders. Rolland Horn said, "Likely that wolf you shot at, and maybe hit, was Old Gray. We don't aim to hurt her on account she's raising a spotted dog pup." Rolland then told Abe he could have work as a rider, but that an effort was being made to get hold of the spotted pup while Old Gray still mothered him. Rolland continued, "There's two black wolves on the range that's plumb bad in killing the cattle and every feller is trying to get 'em with a rifle, but we've quit putting poison in the carcasses on account we don't want to poison that strange dog pup and to tell the truth we have all got a plumb soft spot for Old Gray, the old she-wolf that's trying to raise the pup."

Abe was more than willing to help, he told Rolland and the others. He said with genuine regret, "I hope I didn't hurt the old wolf much, if that was her. It's the first time I ever hated it on account I shot at a gray wolf, but a wolf like this here Old Gray you tell about is different—her trying to raise up a real dog pup. I'm plumb interested. How big is he?"

Matt said, "We don't know for certain on account we ain't seen him now for a month. But we know he's a nice big pup. Old Gray has got a new den for him. We'll keep a watch near the river woods where you shot at her. She may have him hid somewhere near that place."

The next day Matt Henderson, Rolland

Horn and Abe Rivers rode to the place where it was believed Abe had seen Old Gray. It was a long distance from the other den where the traps had been set, but all three riders, knowing gray wolves as they did, were not surprised. They knew it would be quite natural for Old Gray to take her pup a long distance from the other den and try to hide Dusty in a den wholly unknown to the men. Along the margin of the river, in the woods and along the hills on either side, the three cowboys rode for hours, but they did not see a sign of either Old Gray or the spotted pup. Finally Rolland said, "She's got him hid and herself, too. She's an old wolf, one we've known for years, and she's the biggest she-wolf we've ever seen. She's big but awful old and her fangs must be getting dull by now. Maybe the two black wolves would finish her and the pup, too, if they caught them out, but maybe not. If Old Gray was young she'd finish both the black wolves, but with her age and having to look after that purty pup, too, I reckon the old lady must be plumb troubled at times—unless she's already plumb done for.

"And if she is," Rolland went on, "that purty pup wouldn't last a month. He'd get hungry and he'd start out for grub and it would be only a little time till the two black killers would see him and eat him plumb up."

Rolland and Matt and Abe rode on slowly down the river, looking searchingly along the hillsides and the river valley ahead of them. It was a still, warm day. Hardly a breeze stirred. Even the leaves on the cottonwoods were still and the voices of the three riders sounded distinctly in the woods and up the hillside. They rode on and finally out of sight far down the stream where it turned toward the east. For a time after the riders disap-

peared there was stillness all along the hillside. Then something came to life up on the
slope. Among the rocks and stunted trees up
the hill was a little spring that murmured
and tinkled its way out and down the slope.
Old Gray stood up in the shelter here, and
seeing the riders disappear she turned and
drank from the spring. Then she hurried
back to the den.

Fortunately the bullet from Abe Rivers'
rifle had only given Old Gray a flesh wound.
It was not serious and while it smarted a little
it was nothing to her. Dusty was all that mattered. What she feared now was that the men
might find this den, also. Men were cunning.
They were very cunning. Because they rode
away and did not seem to be thinking of you,
meant nothing. In fact when they did this,
very likely you were the one they *were* thinking about.

IV

Clay Banyan

THE more Old Gray lay in the den and thought about the men the more troubled she was over the safety of Dusty. She remained with him all that day and all that night, and many times she licked him affectionately. When she did so the wild look left her eyes and there was something very gentle in them.

Old Gray would have left the den on this night and taken Dusty to a distant point to find another hiding place, but she was afraid the wolves would get him. And when the daylight at last came she was still afraid to

travel because the daytime, she knew, was
when the men were abroad on the wild range.
Still she must choose either the day or the
night, and when the sun was peeping over
the eastern hills she went out of the den and
called Dusty. He came at once and this time
he seemed more than willing to follow her
when she started away toward the northwest.
Old Gray trotted so rapidly that Dusty had
to lope to keep up, but the morning air was
cool and fresh and he felt the thrill and tin-
gle of life as he hurried away with Old Gray.
Dusty did not know where she was going, but
that did not matter to him. All places were
new and strange to him, and at this time he
was timid and afraid of any place whatever.
But he trusted Old Gray. As long as she was
with him life was very good.

Old Gray traveled, for the most part, in
the lowlands where there were deep woods
along the creeks and groves of trees on the

narrow silent valleys. Dusty was so young
that it was not long until he began to grow
tired and, at last, while they moved through
a woods by a stream, he stopped and made a
little sound. Old Gray turned and saw that
he was lying down and panting from his exertion. She lay down with him in the silence
of the cool shady woods and Dusty fell sound
asleep. He slept for two hours. When he
awakened, Old Gray led him on through the
woods. It was a little past noon when she began to be desperately hungry. And when the
hunger pangs gnawed at her great body she
was driven to hunt for food.

She had come out of the woods to the open
land where, not far away, stood a low hill
with many big rocks extending up the slope
and over the summit. Old Gray stopped for
a minute while she looked about her, then
led Dusty up among these rocks on the top
of the hill. There was a pocket under a huge

boulder here, big enough for him to hide in. Old Gray led him to the place and tried to get him to hide there. After a time she got him to understand and he lay down in the shallow place under the boulder.

Old Gray looked quickly all about the place, then started off across the hill for food. Dusty pricked up his ears and watched her. When she disappeared from sight in a dip in the hills he whined and began to whimper to himself. Dusty was doing his best but he was a dog, and the misunderstanding between him and Old Gray was always pulling each of them toward some dangers that would not have existed for them if he had been a young wolf. Old Gray was in the position of a mother hen with a brood of little ducks when they come to water. Strangely enough, however, Old Gray had adopted him and when she gave herself to him she did so with a devotion unsurpassed. And even now while she hurried along in the lowland beyond, searching for food, she did so almost desperately, for she wanted only enough to give her strength so that she might get back and take care of him.

It happened that on this afternoon there was in the neighborhood one of those enemies Old Gray had been trying to get away from, that is—a man on horseback. He was Clay Banyan, a Mexican. Clay was a wandering hunter. In these days he had turned to wolf hunting since some of the cattlemen were paying him for this work. During this spring Clay had established himself in a small log house, used at times by cowboys who were "line riders" at this borderline of the vast ranch.

So it was that while Old Gray had led Dusty into a new region to get away from the men on horses, as she supposed, she had actually led him to a place where there were other riders.

It happened that Clay Banyan rode along the summit of the rocky hill about an hour after Old Gray had left the place. Suddenly Clay pulled his horse to a stop and, as was his habit when excited, he talked aloud to himself. He said: "Well, I be daggoned! That looks something like a young wolf setting out there, but it ain't! It's a dog! A dog pup for sure! Now is he wild or ain't he, and how'd he get here? Well, no matter. I'll get him!"

Clay's quick eyes surveyed the hilltop. There was no place where the pup could hide that he could see. He would run him down if necessary. Clay started the horse forward slowly toward Dusty who, at the moment, was several rods away from the place under the rock where Old Gray had left him. Dusty's back was toward the horseman and so he did not see him. He was sitting down and looking off into the strange mysterious world where Old Gray had disappeared. After the manner of most dogs he could not see far, and even a short distance away, the landscape with its dark woods and rocky hills appeared blurred to him. Suddenly he was startled by the thumping sounds of a horse's hoofs behind him. He turned his head quickly and at once he was badly frightened. Dusty uttered a whining growl and started to run for the pocket under the rock when suddenly the tremendous animal, with the man sitting on its back, began to rush at him. Dusty ran in circles, and he ran desperately for he could not reach the big rock. He was afraid to run away from this place and yet he was fearful to keep running around and around. After a desperate time of this rushing about he was almost exhausted, but at last he reached the shallow pocket under the rock and dived in. He knew at once that he was trapped as he looked out at the man who had now dismounted, squatted down on his heels and, with a grin, looked at his prize.

Clay said, "Well, I be daggoned! A dog pup! Now, I take you with me!" Clay reached slowly under the rock and grabbed so quickly that he had Dusty by the neck before Dusty knew it. He struggled and yelped but it was no use. Clay quickly mounted his horse and, holding Dusty with one arm, he galloped away toward his cabin in the creek woods.

It was but a short time after this that Old Gray came running across the hilltop. She had not found very much food but her concern for Dusty had driven her to return. When she found him gone and the man smell strong at the hiding place under the rock, she was desperate. She had got the man smell even before she reached the place and now she was almost frantic. But to get Dusty again she must be cautious.

Swiftly she ran on in a wide circle, her nose to the ground; then being sure of the scent of the horse, she ran ahead on the trail. And when a little later Clay Banyan put his prize in one corner of the cabin and shut the door, Old Gray had reached a point in the deep shadows of the woods not far from the house. There she hid and set her eyes on the place.

Clay had put Dusty in one corner of the cabin on a horse blanket and dropped some bits of meat on the floor for him to eat, but Dusty only lay in the corner, his eyes wide and frightened. Clay busied himself getting his evening meal, but as he did so, he often looked at Dusty lying in the corner on the blanket. Clay was hungry, and after a time he quit looking at Dusty. It was very unusual to find a dog pup in this manner, but Clay, with his simple mind, took the thing as it came.

After supper Clay sat and smoked his pipe for a time. He talked to Dusty but did not try to touch him again. Then Clay lay down on his bunk and shortly was so sound asleep that he snored.

The door of the cabin was shut but there were two windows, at this time both open, one on either side of the house. The lower sills of these windows were about four feet up from the floor.

Dusty had been too scared to move since he had been put in the corner. The moon shone full into the room now and he was still afraid. He looked up at the sleeping man on the bunk and he heard the rhythmical sounds of Clay's snores.

The truth was that while Clay was a sound sleeper he was, at times, an extremely nervous person. Clay had courage enough, but as one of the cowboys once said of him, "If you can slip up on Clay while he's sound asleep and prod him, he goes up in the air like a mountain cat, and he howls like one, too!" And as it turned out, the thing that happened here on this night was enough to stir even the calmest man to action.

Old Gray waited as long as she could out in the shadows, then, though still more fearful of the man than she was of any other enemy, she stole swiftly and silently up to the house and sniffed at the crack under the closed door. Yes! Dusty was in there. She could smell him and she could both smell and hear the snoring Clay Banyan. Old Gray pushed on the door with a big front foot but she could not move it. She walked around the house and looked up first at the open window above Clay's bunk, then she went around on the opposite side and looked up at the other. Something in her brain made her know she could leap up and through the window as easily as a cat, but she was troubled because she had a feeling that she might not be able to get Dusty and leap out with him. And this was all she wanted. She had no thought of revenge. She just wanted Dusty. Old Gray dreaded the thought of fighting a man. She knew from long experience how helpless she and her kind were in the face of those long dark objects that men carried—the long dark things that cracked and spit fire and many times brought death from a long distance away.

She had no way of knowing that on this night Clay's rifle was on a rack on the opposite side of the room from where he lay snoring. If Old Gray had known this she could have leaped through the open window where she would have stood between Clay and his rifle. With her great size and strength he would have been helpless before her. But she did not want to fight anything, or anybody, on this night. She was only troubled about Dusty and wanted to get him away quickly.

She turned and walked around the house three times and once more she sniffed under the door. Dusty heard the softest of sounds at the door but he was too young to understand. The splash of moonlight in the house broadened and fell full on a wide space on the floor and under the window opposite from Clay.

At last Old Gray could wait no longer. No matter what happened to her she must try to get Dusty out of this place. She stood up on her hind legs, and her head and shoulders were well above the windowsill. The next second she dropped back to the ground and, gathering her powerful muscles, she sprang through the open window, landing on the board floor with a "thump." But Clay snored on. At once she got to Dusty and he began to lick her in his delight. She moved to the window and he followed. Now she must try to get him out!

In the danger and excitement of it all she set her teeth harder than necessary in the back of Dusty's neck, preparatory to leaping outside with him. When she grabbed him, Dusty did the most natural thing for a pup to do—he yelled "Ouch!" in his dog language, and he yelled as loud as he could. The next instant things happened. Clay not only awakened but he sat up with a bounce! He saw, to his amazement, the huge form of a giant wolf at the window—a giant wolf standing on its hind legs with a pup in its mouth! Clay yelled in terror and nobody needed to tell him what to do. He leaped out of the open window by his bunk. Old Gray held Dusty out over the window, dropped him to the ground outside, and swiftly leaped after him. She started running for the woods,

and Dusty, badly frightened, ran with her.
And in his haste he tried to run ahead of her.

Clay saw the two running away. He leaped
back in the cabin, got his rifle, and although
he could see only the last flash of Old Gray
as she plunged into the woods, he fired at her
and kept on shooting blindly in her direction.
Clay was too scared to think about anything
except that he wondered if that wolf *was* as
big as she looked! And Clay, being a super-
stitious individual, ran into the house, locked
the door and the windows, and stayed up all
night. At dawn he rode away and no one in
this region ever saw him again.

It happened that one of the shots struck
Old Gray. It did not strike her fair but went
into the flesh of her front leg, and she stag-
gered as it hit her. But she had neither the
time nor the inclination to think of herself.
This place out here was, to her, even worse
than the one she had left far back on the

other range. She was now going back to the
place she had left. She knew there was danger there also but at least it was an excellent
hiding place for Dusty. She would go back
and take her chances there on the old range.
It was a place where she had lived with her
mate when she was young.

It had been long now since she had tasted
any food to speak of, but she gave it little
thought as she hurried on through the night.
Dusty, in the meantime, hurried on with her.
He was not troubled. In fact he was so young
and his experience with the man had been so
brief that it made little impression on him.

Old Gray at last settled down into a steady
trot and while she traveled through the valley she kept just at the edge of a long belt
of timber where she and Dusty were hidden
in the shadows. Three times on the long jour-
ney Dusty whimpered from hunger. Old
Gray herself was ravenous for food. But she

thought only of him. When she got him back to the old range and safe in a den, she would hunt food. At last she stopped in the open valley and lay down, and as she did so she raised her great head and looked searchingly about for any sign of enemies.

There was not the faintest breeze and the fresh green grass about her bent low with a heavy dew while she looked and listened in the hush of the moonlit night.

V

In the Valley of the Little Cedar

MILES away from the ranch house, in the northwest, there was a lonely place known as the Valley of the Little Cedar. The place got its name because of the one small cedar that grew in the valley not far from the gently flowing stream.

It was about noon, several weeks later, on a still summer day when Old Gray led Dusty out of the woods, where she had been hiding with him, and up to the stream to drink. She was more thirsty than usual on this day and she drank long of the clear cool water. Dusty soon satisfied his thirst. He did not feel the increasing strain of anxiety as did Old Gray. She was old and he was young. At this moment Dusty was hungry. And no matter how much he ate he was hungry again, for he was already big and growing rapidly. After he had lapped all the water he wanted he stood looking across the stream, the water dripping from his jaws. He saw nothing to make him afraid, yet he was uneasy. Three times in the last two weeks he and Old Gray had come dangerously near the two black wolves, but each time some kind of den was available where Old Gray got him in to safety.

Although the two black wolves would have tried to drive Old Gray from the range or destroy her even if she had been alone, they were more deadly than ever when they saw her with the big spotted pup. Each time Old Gray ran with Dusty into a den, the two black wolves went near and sniffed with noses pointing in the direction of the dark opening and then slunk away. While they sensed, from a few skirmishes with Old Gray a year before, that she could no longer fight like a younger wolf, they nevertheless knew her spirit, and they would not attack her unless they could both rush together. Old Gray was larger than either of them. That would help, but her age was against her.

At last Old Gray stopped drinking. She turned about and started away from the stream toward the high bluffs on the east, expecting to go up to the summit. Dusty, as usual, was behind her when both stopped dead in their tracks. Loping around a spur of the bluff ran the two black wolves. For a second the two wolves were as much surprised as Old Gray, then they rushed at her and Dusty.

Old Gray, at the same time, ran to get

Dusty out of danger. She knew he was too young to stand against these two rushing black beasts. If she could get him safe in a den she did not care what happened. She would whirl and face both her enemies, with all the contempt of her being.

Dusty ran behind Old Gray as hard as he could but the black wolves were gaining swiftly. If Old Gray had been alone here it is probable she could have saved herself somehow, but she could never leave Dusty. As she ran she looked desperately for some point of vantage where she might protect him from these enemies. She got Dusty part way up the hill to a little level grassy place, surrounded on three sides by a mass of boulders. And as Old Gray rushed into the place, she saw an opening on the hill under one of the boulders. In a flash her wolf instinct told her Dusty could get in the den even if she couldn't. When Old Gray saw the hole under the rock she supposed he would dart in there. But again Dusty astonished her in not acting like a young gray wolf of his age.

She just had time to whirl and face her enemies as they drove at her. She fell upon them with such fury that she repelled their first attack, but she got two severe wounds in her side. Here Dusty surprised Old Gray. She had forgotten him, but he had not gone in the hole. She now heard a snarl beside her and there stood Dusty, hair standing on his neck, a wild greenish light in his eyes, as he looked at the wolves.

He was not seven months old but he was very big for a pup. He must have weighed at least seventy-five pounds, yet he was still a pup in experience. At the first rush of the wolves Dusty and Old Gray were both cut, and Dusty was so badly hurt he could hardly stand. But he was ready to fight. The two black beasts charged in and Old Gray met them with everything she had. And again she was seriously wounded, but she slashed both her enemies severely, and for a moment they stood back, their heads down, panting.

Again the black wolves rushed in and this time an unfortunate thing happened. Old Gray met them with a terrific drive, but the effort carried her beyond the cover of the rocks and in that second Dusty was out with her and he was slashing and fighting with all the fighting blood of his wolfhound ancestors. Twice again he was cut but he only fought the harder. Dusty would almost certainly have gone down but for the merest accident.

The battle between the two black wolves and Old Gray and Dusty was raging furiously when Matt Henderson rode up on the bluff above. Matt was quick of eye and hand. He saw everything at once. He jerked his rifle from the holster on the saddle, dismounted, threw his bridle reins over a tall rock, bent down on one knee and fired. The female black wolf went down. Matt fired again quickly, but the male black wolf rushed away and escaped. Matt mounted his horse and rode down the hill. There he saw Old Gray drag herself up the slope toward the little enclosure among the rocks. Then she fell and just lay there on the grass, close to Dusty. Matt came up. He saw that Dusty had his head up but Old Gray's head was down on the grass. As Matt came close he saw her raise her head, lick Dusty once on his head, then she fell back and Old Gray was gone.

Matt stood and looked in amazement. Dusty was badly slashed. And his wild up-bringing now showed itself. He saw the wounded dog drag himself into the den under the rock. Somehow it did not occur to Matt to stop him. It seemed best to leave

Dusty alone. But after Dusty had disappeared Matt thought maybe he had made a mistake. Perhaps he should have got hold of him and tried to restrain him, but after all he could not have got this big young dog to the ranch without help. If Dusty was wounded badly enough to die, Matt believed it would be soon. But he might live because he was so young. Then a happy thought came to Matt. Dusty was safe, at least, from the other black wolf, that is if Dusty would stay in the den and have food and water. Matt, with the help of Rolland and the others, would do this much for Dusty. They would get food and water to him here. Matt got down and looked in the dark den. Far back he could see what looked like two balls of fire and he was certain that Dusty was alive and looking at him. Of course it would be foolish to call to a wild dog and expect him to come out. So Matt left at once and he looked up and down the river hoping to see some of the men, but found that he was alone in the valley.

He thought to himself there was no use in waiting. He might as well ride to the ranch house and bring back some food for Dusty. Also, he would bring a bucket for water. Dusty, being badly wounded, would need water more than anything else. The river was not far from his den. It would be easy to carry the water up in the bucket and put it under the rock. And the water should be put in the den as soon as possible. Otherwise Dusty might crawl out and go to the river where the black wolf might find him.

Matt got to his horse and rode home at a swift pace. Rolland was at the ranch house— had just gotten in. Both Rolland and old Ben, the cook, listened in surprise at Matt. Then Rolland said, "You're right, Son. Water must be got to that young dog in a hurry. Creatures that's bad hurt always want lots of water. I'll go along."

Mounted on fresh horses, they started back. Old Ben had given Matt a small tin bucket and this, with a generous portion of meat, was tied on the saddle. As Matt and Rolland rode swiftly across the high table-land few words were spoken. Their thoughts were on the wounded dog.

While Matt had stood at the den the thought had come to him that he might carry rocks to the place and so stop Dusty from coming out, but he believed no animal, not even the black wolf, would dare go into a den where a dog as big as Dusty lay. It would be best, Matt thought, to leave the den open so that Dusty would not become frightened, thinking he could never get out. With these thoughts in mind Matt rode steadily on with Rolland across the highlands and finally down in the wild rough country cut through with deep ravines and lonely rocky gorges. Then the night fell and the bright stars shone upon riders and galloping horses. The wind that had sprung up an hour earlier had died away and the western night was still as the two horses galloped along. Now and then the horses struck a patch of small loose stones and the rocks clattered under their hoofs, and now and then the fire flew as a horse's hoof struck the stones.

As Matt and Rolland rode rapidly on they saw here and there in front, and on either side of them, huge, gray, silent boulders standing in the lonely night. Once Matt's horse snorted when a big coyote ran from the shadows of one of the big rocks. But Matt paid little attention. His mind was on the wounded wild dog that the cowboys called Dusty.

Would Dusty remain safe in the den away out here on the range until Matt brought food and water to him? Matt feared that, wounded as he was, he might feel the pangs of thirst so much that he might come out and try to get down to the river.

VI

Dusty Leaves the Den

Dusty lay in the dark den for a long time after Matt rode away toward the distant ranch house, and now the night had come. Dusty could not know what was in the mind of Matt. All he knew was that he felt a terribly increasing thirst for water. He sensed the danger to himself if he went outside his shelter for he knew the black wolf might be near. But at last his thirst became unbearable. Slowly he got to the opening of the den and slowly he moved out a little until he had his head outside in the open air. This revived

him a little and he lay for a brief time and
looked at the river below. He saw only the
silent starlit slope between him and the river,
and the thirst for water urged him on. He
moved out a little, looking searchingly
around him in the meantime, until at last he
was outside the den. After sniffing the air and
looking intently, before him he crawled a
little way down the slope and then on to the
margin of the valley. There he stopped, panting. The green grass was already laden with
dew and as he moved on he licked his long
tongue over the grass to get what moisture he
could. He paused again and again and once
he uttered a whine of utter misery. He was
desperate for water.

At last Dusty reached the river and began
lapping the water. It seemed he would never
get enough, but finally he turned and started
slowly up the slope. As he moved on and up
he passed near the form of Old Gray. He had

passed by her when he started for the river but he was suffering so much for water that he had thought of nothing else. Now he thought only of her. Badly cut and bleeding as he was, he forgot about himself. He moved slowly along beside the still form of Old Gray and licked her a few times, then cried lowly in his longing for her to come back. He wanted her so that all would be as it was before. But in some way he could see that this could never be. He stood by her for a time, looking first one way then the other and out on the valley. He was not looking for help, for he knew there was none and he hardly knew what he did. After a little time he lay down very close to Old Gray with his head on the ground, and although his eyes were half open he saw nothing and he cared for nothing. He breathed a long quivering breath and a low sound escaped him. In one way nature seemed kind to him here for no enemy appeared. A low breeze whispered and sighed along the grass of the hillside and only the stars looked down on the scene in the lonely valley. For a long time Dusty lay as still as the rocks around him. At last he slowly got to his feet and slowly he started for the den. He knew the world had suddenly changed for him. It was very strange, and he knew that from this time he must go on alone. He did not know how, but there was no other way.

Slowly he moved up the slope. At times he stopped and panted from this little exertion, but he moved on and at last reached the opening of the den. His wounds were bleeding badly now. Somehow he got inside, where he fell—unconscious. As time passed he was vaguely aware of the place he was in, but again things faded away and he lived in a land of troubled dreams.

Inside the den was only the silence, darkness, and he who lay so still. Outside the wind had died down and there was a hush in the starlit night.

Dusty had no way of knowing how long he lay here, but day had come. He was aroused by many sounds that at first were dim and vague to him. Presently, as he looked toward the shaft of light at the opening of the den, he could see moving forms and a little later he saw the arm of a man move into the den and he could smell something that he knew was food. He saw what seemed many movements at the opening and presently something else was put inside the den beside the food, and Dusty's nose told him it was water. Again this was the thing above all else that he wanted and, even though he had drunk long at the river, he felt an urge to crawl at once to the water near the opening of the den.

Matt had arrived and carefully set a

bucket full of water, and some raw beef, in the den. Rolland had told Matt to use raw beef since it was certain that the wild Dusty had never tasted cooked meat and so he would like the raw meat better.

After what seemed a long time to Dusty the sounds outside died away and deep stillness fell on the place. More and more Dusty wanted to crawl to the water and after some time had passed he could wait no longer. He crawled from the darkness at the rear toward the opening, stopping at times to listen, and after a time he reached the bucket of water. Instantly he began to lap the life-giving fluid and he drank until he could hold no more. Having finished, he picked up one of the pieces of beef and took it to the back of the den where he dropped it. As yet he was not hungry. Time was nothing to Dusty here. He lay perfectly still for an hour, looking intently at the light near the opening. He was not hungry but nature made him know he would be later. Again he crawled to the front part of the den and this time he moved back and forth until he had carried all the meat to the rear. He then lay exhausted and, closing his eyes, he soon fell asleep.

During the first three days that Dusty lay in the den he was so weak from loss of blood that he slept much and drank frequently of the water from the bucket that was set in for him every day by Matt. He ate very little during that time. But at the end of three days he began to be hungry and at the end of a week he was getting strong. When ten days had gone by Dusty was again keen and alert and one afternoon he watched with shining eyes when Matt brought food and water and set them in the dark den. Matt had not failed to come each day, and every day it was the same. He brought water and meat.

During the first days Rolland Horn and

Charley Stone came along with Matt to see if the wild young dog was still in the den, but on the fourth morning Rolland said to Matt, "Well, Son, I don't know how it will come out, but one thing is certain, this wild Dusty dog is sure drinking the water and eating the meat you are taking to him. Of course it's plumb natural for him to do this but it will be an awful mess if it turns out that you are raising up a dog to be as big as a calf and one that takes a notion to run with that black wolf and help him kill the cattle."

Charley spoke up, saying, "Now, Rolland, you watch! Although this Dusty is a wild dog, he's dog and nothing but dog, and my guess is that when he gets his growth, unless the black wolf gets him before that time, why, this here Dusty will be plumb unsociable with that same wolf and if he meets up with him some day all alone out on the range, why, Dusty, remembering what that black wolf done to him and Old Gray, will start in on him and scatter him over the landscape until buzzards can't hardly find him."

During these days that Matt took meat and water to the distant den Rolland Horn and the other men talked with Matt about plans to capture Dusty. One day, when Matt had come with Rolland and Charley to the den, Rolland had carefully looked at the ground around the place with the thought of building a high wire fence. But it was found that a few inches below the earth lay what seemed almost solid rock. The idea of a fence was therefore given up. Matt spoke once of blocking the opening of the den with big rocks so that when Dusty wanted to come out he would know he was a prisoner.

At this Rolland said, "Matt, I wouldn't do that. If you do Dusty would become plumb scared and he'd know you and the rest of us did the work and he'd be more scared of us all than ever. The best way is to keep right on as you are. Keep bringing water and meat to him and each time you come to the den, lay down in front of the place and look in and talk kind to him. He won't know what you say but he sure will know that the stuff you are bringing him is plumb good, and being a young dog, he'll just naturally get interested in the feller that's so good to him when he's in so much trouble. Of course I don't say I *know* he'll feel that way, but knowing dogs, I know that a dog, and especially a big pup that's hungry, sure gets awful strong for the feller that feeds him. And while Dusty is a wild dog now, he's still a dog and I figure it will work out as I say. Even if he comes out of the den and gets out on the range, which I figure he'll do, he's going to think about you a good deal and he knows you by scent right now. And if he disappears from the den it will mean he has got out on

his own and it will mean plenty of danger
for him, too, with that daggone big black
wolf still running free. So let things take
their course. I got one idea about capturing
him. You remember when Charley and me
roped that daggone mountain lion that was
out in the valley near Buffalo Springs? Remember how we roped it and put a stop to it
killing the colts? Well, if Charley and me
can rope a thing like that I figure that if we
ever come up on Dusty where he can't get
away we can rope him. But you mustn't be
with us at the time and you must never do
anything that would scare him. You must be
different to him."

"That suits me," Matt said. "I think he's
not as much afraid of me right now as he was
the first time I went to the den. And yester-
day, when I put the meat in the den and
talked to him, he didn't stay away back in
the den as before but crawled halfway out to-

ward that meat. Of course it was the meat he was so hungry for, but it showed he was getting less afraid of me."

"Exactly," said Rolland. "And now don't be discouraged if you go there and find him gone just any time. When his wounds heal and he can travel I figure he'll take a chance on running free. If he does, and finally gets to be a cattle killer, that will be bad. But being a young dog, he's going to remember you and in time, my guess is he'll want more and more to be pretty close to you so he can eat and drink when he wants to, and also because there's something in his nature he can't get rid of—something that will make him want to be with a human like you all the time."

Charley Stone said, "It might be so, but it looks to me like Dusty might not grow up, him being in plenty of danger if he gets out on the range again, on account of that savage black wolf."

Rolland grinned and said, "That wolf will have to hurry on account Dusty's legs are too long, him being like a big wolfhound. When he gets in good shape again he can run away from that wolf like a puff of smoke. If Dusty lives, my guess is that some day it will be a race but it will be a race where Dusty is running hard trying to get that black wolf."

VII

Night

THE moon was up, shining on hill and valley. A low wind was blowing from the south, and just outside the den in which Dusty lay, it made a whispering sound in the nearby thickets. Dusty had crawled to the mouth of the den and for a short time he lay with his head out, looking and listening.

After a time he crawled outside and stood up while he looked down the slope toward the river. There was nothing to be seen but the big naked rocks and a cedar tree with deep mysterious shadows beneath its spreading branches.

Dusty stood, for a little, sniffing the air. It was fresh, and already he felt new life in him. His wounds were fairly well healed, and being young he was again very strong. As he stood outside in the moonlight looking about him for enemies, he thought mainly of the dangerous black wolf. Dusty feared him, knowing he was no match for him now. But at the same time nature made Dusty sure of his legs. He was not afraid of being caught by the black wolf unless the beast leaped upon him suddenly from behind some rock or thicket. But Dusty's mind was not wholly on the black wolf. He thought, also, of the kindly youth that had brought food and water to him in his trouble. The truth was that on this night, when Dusty crawled outside of the den, he was to leave it for good. He had decided that he wanted to find a hiding place near the youth that had brought food and water. Not that Dusty would come up to Matt. He would not do this, because he was still afraid. But he wanted to get nearer the place where Matt was. Strange thought it was, it was fine to be near Matt. Inside the den that Dusty had just left stood the bucket with a little water in it, but Dusty had eaten the meat.

It had happened that Matt had been later than usual this day in riding to the den. It was sunset when he rode away. This was all the better for Dusty. He began to smell the ground carefully. He got the scent of Matt where he had been close to the opening of the den and had talked low to Dusty. Matt had done this each day. Dusty worked his way down the slope still smelling the scent of Matt, then he came to the place where he had got on his horse, and here Dusty carefully smelled the footprints of the horse. There must be no mistake about this since there were other horses traveling on the range. To follow Matt's trail Dusty would have to follow that of the horse, and he understood. He started off on the trail and followed at an angle up the slope and finally reached the high tableland that stretched away for miles toward the south. And here on this highland Dusty found Matt's trail leading southward, and continuing on in this direction.

Dusty ran on as best he could. He was not the kind of dog who could scent a trail like a foxhound, but he had a good enough nose to follow the trail with certainty. At times the trail led over rocky flats on the highland, but Dusty only worked the harder because of this, and by running in wide circles when he lost the trail, he invariably picked it up a little farther on. After he had followed the trail across the highlands for miles he found it turned sharply down into a long wide valley stretching on toward the south. Dusty stopped, stood on the high ground, and looked anxiously out on the bright moonlit valley below him. He saw the level land stretching before him, with here and there clumps of tall trees standing like dark silent shadows. After looking for a time, and seeing no moving thing below him, he hurried down the slope, still following the trail of Matt's horse.

Down in the valley the trail led on past many clumps of trees and here and there a small thicket. As Dusty ran on, his nose to the ground, he felt thirst and began to look about him for water. Not far away in a depression in the valley he got a scent that led him to a pool of water which was bordered by tall slough grass and straggling willow trees. Dusty trotted to the slough, a little distance away, and when he reached the edge of the grass, he found a place where the cattle had made a trail as they came in to drink. He walked noiselessly over the muddy trail and came down to the water. As he drank, Dusty looked across on the silent water and also on either side of him. He realized now that no one could help him but himself. Three times he stopped lapping the water and looked behind him on the trail that led through the tall grass. But he saw no animal and he heard nothing but the wind rustling through the tall slough grass on either side of him. He stood for a minute in the moonlight, listening, then he turned and moved cautiously out to the open land. He found the trail of Matt's horse again and this time he ran more eagerly than ever. The cool of the night and the water he had drunk put life in his young body and he felt strong.

The scent of Matt's horse was so faint at times that Dusty had to stop and sniff for a little time to be certain. But he managed to

keep the scent until he reached a point where
Matt had ridden over a long stretch of almost solid rock bordering a stream. Here
Dusty lost the trail and he spent some time in
search of it. Twice he ran to the stream's
edge and looked across at the dark woods on
the other side and he uttered an anxious
whine. Then he ran along the long rocky
margin of the stream and on until he was
across the place, when in the scattering woods
he again found the trail. He gave a whine of
joy as he ran. Presently the trail opened out
of the woods along the stream and out on a
vast region of rolling plains that led toward
the south. Dusty ran across the open land in
the moonlight, his white- and dusty-colored
body the only moving thing on this sea of
wild range land. He did not know that it was
not more than five miles to the ranch house
of the Rolland Horn ranch.

Suddenly Dusty stopped. He stopped and

shrank back quickly as if startled by a rattlesnake. But it was not a snake that startled
him. It was the scent of the black wolf.
And the scent was strong. He instinctively
dropped close to the ground and lay in the
moonlight for a few seconds. If the black
wolf was near, Dusty wanted to see him before the enemy saw Dusty. But there was no
big black animal in sight. All that Dusty
could see was the dim plain ahead of him.
He was deeply concerned at being out in the
open with no possible hiding place at a time
like this. Certainly the black wolf had been
here, and not long before. At last Dusty got
to his feet and started forward on Matt's
trail. To his great surprise and concern he
found that the trail of the black wolf led
along the trail of Matt. Dusty stopped and
sat down. He did not want to trail the black
enemy and yet he could not avoid this if he
followed the trail of Matt.

Dusty now moved along the trail with the utmost caution. He would run forward, then stop, look intently ahead of him, and run on again. He had gone some two miles in this way, with the scent of the black wolf's tracks alongside the trail of Matt's horse, when Dusty saw, not far forward, the shadowy forms of many trees. But the trail led on and Dusty followed it cautiously. He came to a long line of dark woods along a sandy stream. Here Dusty smelled the trail carefully. He got the scent of Matt's horse again, but at this point he could not smell the footprints of the black wolf. He walked slowly to one side and after making a circle he found the trail of the wolf. It seemed to lead directly away from Matt's trail. Had the wolf gone off? Dusty tried to decide. He stood for a minute listening intently and at the same time trying to see any moving thing in the open spaces among the trees along the river.

But he could neither smell nor see anything that warned him of the enemy's presence.

Dusty walked on into the woods while watching constantly. Old Gray was no longer with him. It was different now and Dusty knew the danger. He crossed through the woods where the moonlight shone through the leafy trees and down upon him as he moved watchfully through the open spaces. Whenever it was difficult to see at a distance, he would stop and stand very still. As he moved along, a little breeze sprang up, and as it went past him toward the stream he heard the rustling of the many leaves on the trees and even this made him watch and listen, but nothing could be seen and he went on until he reached the sandy margin of the water. Dusty stopped and looked up the stream a little distance at a thicket, but seeing no sign of enemies, he walked down to drink.

He lapped only a little water and turned

back to search for Matt's trail. Then, with not the least warning, a big black form shot around the thicket and before Dusty could get in action the savage black wolf was almost upon him. Dusty leaped with all his might straight out into the shallows of the stream. Swiftly he crossed the shallows, and plunged into water over his depth.

The black wolf had rushed hard. He plunged into the deep water behind and for a moment both were swimming. Dusty quickly reached the shallows on the other side, and although the enemy was close behind him he would have escaped without a scratch but for a big pile of driftwood directly in front of him. Dusty whirled to the right and darted like a rabbit around the drift. By this move the black wolf had rushed close and slashed Dusty slightly on the hip, but before the wolf could snap again Dusty was around the drift and in the clear

on the other side. Young dog that he was, he
was of a breed noted for both speed and endurance, and he knew he was running for his
life.

When he reached the level grassland beyond the stream, Dusty ran so swiftly he soon
widened the gap between him and his enemy.
He reached a turn in the valley and got completely away from the wolf by running into
the darkness of a hillside, densely covered
with trees. In this dark shelter Dusty made
his way to the open highland far above and
there slowed down to a trot. He had lost the
trail of Matt's horse, but since it had led
south Dusty now moved in that direction.

He stopped once, and licked the place
where the wolf had bit him. Having done
this, Dusty stood up, looked back on the trail,
and something of his ancestors showed in
him. The hair on his neck stiffened and he
throated a deep growl. He was young and in-

experienced, but there was a growing spirit in him that said plainly, "Black wolf, beware!"

Dusty had gone less than two miles when he made a discovery that pleased him greatly, although it made him even more cautious. On reaching the rim of a low hill he looked down on the level and saw, surprisingly near, the dark form of a ranch house standing among some trees. At the same time he smelled horses and heard one of them squeal in a big corral below. Dusty cocked his ears and watched for a minute, then stole down the slope and started forward, keeping as close as he could in the shadows of the trees about the place. At last he stood within a few yards of the house itself. He was in the deep shadows of a big tree, and because of this excellent cover he was not very afraid. After looking intently at the house for a time and seeing no sign of life he put his nose down

and sniffed the ground in the shadows under
the tree. He had not yet scented the trail of
Matt, but all at once he scented the horse.
Pointing his nose toward the scent, Dusty
found the animal standing and dozing in one
of the stables. The horse saw Dusty and
snorted loudly in fear. Dusty got away
quickly.

As he did this, he got a scent that meant
more than all else to him. A little breeze flut-
tered the leaves of a tree beneath which he
stood, and brought to him a scent he had been
trying to find. It was that of the youth who,
when Dusty lay wounded in the den, had put
food and water in to him. Slowly Dusty stole
up through the shadows toward the room
where Matt lay sleeping. The window was
open.

Yes, this certainly was the place where this
good human stayed! Now, to find a hiding
place somewhere near him. He had always

brought food. Maybe there was food to be found near him now. At this moment a delicious scent came to Dusty's nose. He looked intently at the room with the open window, then hurried off to the delicious scent. On this night, as usual, old Ben, as the ranch cook was known, had thrown his table scraps out. Dusty found many beef bones, scraps of meat and pieces of hard bread, all of which he ate rapidly. When he had eaten all he could find he took another look at the house and made his way across the narrow creek behind the stables. Just behind these stables was a deep rocky cut known among the cattlemen as Cougar Gorge. The north slope of this gorge was high with many stunted trees, together with huge dark rocks and great ledges, all of which made an excellent cover for Dusty.

It was nearly morning when he found a dark den that suited him and at once he went in. He had selected a place in a rocky ledge that was so sheltered he could easily look down on the ranch house and all who moved about there, but none could see him. He would hide here, and here he would feast at night from the delicious food to be found near the house, and here he would not be in much danger of the deadly black wolf. That savage beast would be afraid of the men. Dusty could, at his ease, study the one man who had brought him food and water. He would be afraid to come up to this human but there was something irresistible about the youth.

And so it was that the next morning Dusty lay at the mouth of his den and watched not only Matt but all the men. He could hear their voices and he could see all they did. Neither Matt nor a man on the place would have believed it if they had been told that Dusty had his home almost in their backyard.

And while Dusty wanted to stay where he was, he was as careful and watchful as the wildest wolf. For the time being he simply wanted to hide here and then, when several hours of the night had gone by, Dusty would go down and get the delicious food. His main care would be that none of the men should see him either by day or night.

VIII

In Cougar Gorge

DUSTY hid in the den among the rocks and bushes high up on the north side of Cougar Gorge until spring, and not once was he seen by the men. Dusty was cunning. He did not leave the immediate vicinity of the den at all except at night and then only after the light had gone out in the ranch house and he had looked for some time at the darkened place in the silent shadows among the trees.

Fortunately for Dusty it was one of those unusually mild winters in the West when very little snow fell and the sun shone warm and balmy almost every day. There came the peaceful cawing of the crows in the ravines, and the clear whistle of the redbirds could be heard in the woods along the river to the west.

During these days old Ben seemed to limp more than ever because of a crippled foot, and Matt generously assisted him in many ways, one of which was to carry out the table scraps each night and throw them near one of the stables close to the woods of Cougar Gorge. Matt would have been astonished if he had known that Dusty, whom he thought about so often, was actually hiding in the deep shadows of the woods, ready and waiting for the food. At these times Dusty's big young body was so ravenous for food he could hardly wait. But each time he was as quiet as the shadows in which he lay and he waited until Matt had gone back and entered the ranch house.

So it was that while Matt rode far and wide over the range during these mild days hunting for some sign of Dusty, he found none. Nevertheless, he was contributing daily to Dusty's growth, for beef was cheap and table scraps were generous. And the growth of Dusty, when spring came, was surprising. He was now more than a year old, standing full thirty-four inches high at the shoulders and weighing more than one hundred and forty pounds.

One bright moonlit night, this spring, Matt awakened and lay looking out into the shadows cast by the trees near the stables. Something had awakened him, some unusual sound it seemed, but he knew not what. Matt lay looking out in the moonlight and the shadows, aware of the ordinary sounds out there—a snort from one of the horses and the sound of their hoofs as they moved about in the corral. After this there was silence and

only the shadows in the moonlight. But all of
a sudden Matt opened his eyes wide and sat
up on the edge of the bed. He could hardly
believe his eyes! What he saw was Dusty,
much bigger than before. But it was he!
Matt was certain. He saw him come out of
the shadows near the stables and, after looking intently toward the house for a minute,
move up to a place near the stables where
Matt had thrown out the table scraps. Matt
could hear the crack of the beef bones as
Dusty crunched them in his powerful jaws.

Matt knew he saw something here that the
other men would want to see also. Here was
Dusty, the wild dog, within a stone's throw,
and seemingly as calm as if he was a domestic dog! As Matt looked at him he wondered
why Dusty came up so close to the house.
Then it came to him that Dusty might have
a hiding place around somewhere in the deep
Cougar Gorge. Being a real dog and, as the

men had so often said, "nothing but dog,"
Matt thought Dusty might believe the men
were not as dangerous as the black wolf out
on the range. As yet it was a fact that Dusty
had never been hurt by any of the men. The
only thing that made him afraid of them was
that they were wholly strange to him. As
Matt sat on the edge of his bed and watched
Dusty return to the table scraps, all this went
through his mind. Matt thought that it was
probable Dusty was less afraid to take his
chances here near the ranch than out on the
range. Certainly he had reason to know the
black wolf was deadly dangerous because of
what had happened. An intelligent young
dog could not forget. One thing Matt did
not know. This was that in spite of all that
Old Gray had tried to each Dusty, she could
not teach him to have the same fear of men
that she had. It was true that he did fear
them, but he had something in him that Old

Gray never had. This was a deep curiosity about the men. He liked to keep close to them and watch them, while under cover.

This curiosity came over Dusty now and he was especially curious about the youth who had, months ago, put food and water in the den. The youth was now inside the house where the open window was. Dusty finished eating and stood looking at the house in the silence and moonlight. For a minute he looked, then decided to walk up nearer. Matt's heart quickened as he sat on the bed and watched. On came the large spotted dog, slowly, watchfully, in the still night. And the moon shone full on Dusty as he walked slowly forward. Nearer, and nearer still he came, and Matt almost held his breath when Dusty came closer to the open window, his nose in this direction, and sniffed the air. He could not see Matt sitting in the shadows of the room but he got the scent of him. All was silent about the place.

Dusty sat down facing the open window, sat for a little time and looked. Once he uttered the faintest of sounds. The youth who had fed him was in there. Dusty had an overwhelming desire to go up very close to the window, and he slowly went forward until he stood very near. Something deep in him made him want to *belong* here. His long ancestry made this a part of him. He stood there for a brief time and looked. Again came the low sound from him, a distinct whine that told how he felt.

Then he trotted back to the place where he had found the food. After sniffing over the ground again he went near one of the stables and stood looking, until one of the horses snorted loudly. Matt, still watching, saw Dusty dodge back, stand for a minute and look toward the house, then turn and trot down a slope to the north, where he disappeared among the shadows.

Because Dusty had had a good meal he wanted to exercise his fast-growing body and, instead of turning toward his den, he loped past the tall trees toward the west. Dusty was young but of great size now and he had confidence in his strength. He did not know that Matt had seen everything, and that at the moment he was sitting on his bed wide awake, with a scheme already forming to capture Dusty.

When Matt went back to sleep that night, dreaming about his scheme to trap the wild dog, Dusty felt the urge to take a long run through the night, simply for the thrill he got out of running free. He could run from enemies if necessary, but Dusty, with his fangs already long and his strong body, was the kind of dog when fully grown that would be a dangerous antagonist to almost any animal of the wild.

Dusty had run five miles on this night when just as he was loping down a valley near some bushes he stopped short. He got the scent of his dangerous enemy, the black wolf. Suddenly the wolf ran out of a nearby creek bed in the valley and was almost upon Dusty. The surprise was mutual. The big wolf rushed and slashed at Dusty but missed, and Dusty leaped away. Only Dusty's legs could save him at this time. If he would live he must run, and he did. He ran as hard as his legs would carry him, and for a quarter of a mile the black wolf, determined on his destruction, kept close to him. But the wolf did not have the speed of this young wolfhound and Dusty got away from the beast. When Dusty reached some woods along a river, he quickly got out of sight by running into the deep shadows among the trees. Farther up the river he came out of the woods and, with the moon shining upon him, he sat down and looked back in the direction where he had seen his enemy.

On this night, while he sat on the wild plain in the moonlight, he looked for a time toward the dark woods down the river, and instead of a puppy whine there came the deep rumbling growl of a young but nearly grown wolfhound. Three times came the deep growl and the last time it ended in a warning snarl. Dusty had scarcely known his own mother, but he had known Old Gray. He never had been able to understand her and when he was very young she had, at times, frightened him a little. But as he had grown older this fear of her had left him and he understood her. It was just her way of trying to protect him. She was his friend in everything. And tonight, in a vague way, he remembered much that had passed, but in particular he remembered the battle when Old Gray had gone down before the two black wolves. He had been hurt that night and he had gone in the den alone. It was not the same now. Time had made a change.

Dusty got up and started at a lope over the wild range, and as he ran he traveled in a vast circle, for he had in mind to return again to his home in the den high up in Cougar Gorge, above the ranch house.

Where Dusty went that night Matt did not know, but he believed Dusty would return again for the table scraps thrown out at night. For the time, Matt did not tell what he had seen. He thought to himself it would be best not to tell because some of the men might also watch and Dusty might be frightened away. But Matt decided he would tell old Ben. Ben had lived long on the range and had hunted and trapped many wild animals. Old Ben might have a workable scheme for trapping Dusty if he knew that the dog came in the yard at night for food.

IX

Dusty and the Black Wolf

DUSTY lay in his den on this morning looking down at the ranch house. Many times he had seen men outside in the yard and heard their talk and laughter. And many times when the wind blew toward him he got the scent of Matt, and then he would raise his head, cock his ears and show an unusual interest. Dusty got so familiar with this that he could distinguish Matt when he rode away alone. After all these days had gone by here, Dusty would become restless when he saw Matt down by the stables and his eyes would shine with a warm glow because he wanted to go down there where Matt was, but he was still afraid.

It was on the morning after Matt had seen Dusty that Dusty saw Matt mount his horse and ride away from the ranch alone. At once he became unusually restless. He whined and got up from behind the thicket and moved to the west edge of it to watch Matt as he rode farther and farther away. At last Matt and his horse seemed only a dim blur on the far horizon and Dusty could no longer stay where he was. He was a big dog now and had his full growth as to height but he would in time grow heavier. He had tall and big, powerful legs. His coat was long and shaggy, and as he stood behind the thicket looking toward the disappearing Matt in the west, he looked like a dangerous foe to man or beast. It was only the look in his eyes that told how he felt toward the disappearing horseman. In Dusty's eyes was something fine, a look of longing that could not be expressed. And though Dusty had been mothered by a devoted old she-wolf, he was not only a dog but one that came from a strain of dogs that for generations had known only devotion to men. As Dusty stood looking at the retreating Matt, he knew he was the youth that had been kind to him after what had happened that day in the Valley of the Little Cedar.

And so, while Dusty had never felt the friendly touch of a human being upon him, he was irresistibly drawn to the one who was going farther and farther away into the west. Dusty made a low sound and looked quickly toward the ranch house. He saw other riders there setting forth on their horses but none of them were riding toward the west. Dusty decided at once that he would take a chance; he too would travel into the west and follow Matt. As he started out he felt a new strength

and a new confidence. True, he lacked experience, but he was no longer afraid of wild
animals on the range, not even the black
wolf. He knew he was in some danger but
he knew he was strong. He started along the
side of the gorge and kept under cover of the
leafless thickets and behind the big rocks until
he reached a point where the gorge turned
sharply to the north. Dusty knew that at this
point he could not be seen from the ranch
house. Arrived here, he ran down to the open
land below and then raced like a streak across
the same ground that Matt had passed over
only a short time before.

Dusty had covered several miles when,
coming out of a wooded slope, he saw directly ahead of him a high sandy bank with
a cut made by a cattle trail. He heard, then,
something that made him leap swiftly to one
side, where he hid in some dense brush. What
he heard below the high bank at the river was

a human voice, and then Dusty saw Matt ride
up from the cut in the bank and out on the
valley. Matt rode within ten feet of Dusty
without knowing it, and he would not have
been any the wiser but for his horse, who
looked toward the thicket, snorted and
plunged wildly to one side, almost unseating
Matt. Matt got the horse in hand and tried
to ride up to see what it was in the bushes
that scared the horse, but the animal plunged
so violently Matt could not force him up to
the thicket. He did manage to ride clear
around the place while looking sharply in
among the leafy branches. Suddenly he was
thrilled. He saw, lying in the thicket, as quiet
as the green leaves around him, the form of
Dusty—big, powerful, with his dusty and
white coat.

Matt wondered if he should ride a distance up the river where there were some
trees, tie his horse to the tree and come back

on foot. However, he believed this would only frighten Dusty. Then Matt had an idea. He was sure Dusty had not been in this thicket when he rode his horse down to water because the horse had passed close to the thicket and paid no attention to it. Plainly then Dusty had run across the open space between here and a timbered slope beyond while Matt was down at the river's edge giving his horse water. Had Dusty purposely done this to watch Matt? Did he remember Matt's kindness at the den after that day Old Gray had gone down? All this went through Matt's mind. He decided on a ruse. He would find out if Dusty was interested enough to follow him.

Accordingly Matt rode away at a jog trot up the river and acted as if he had nothing in mind but to keep his horse moving forward. All the time, however, he kept his head turned enough so that he could see if Dusty left the thicket. Nothing happened until Matt was a considerable distance up the river where there was a heavy growth of woods along the stream. Matt rode quickly into this cover, dismounted, tied his horse to a tree, and watched the thicket down by the river. He waited for some time and nothing happened. Then his heart quickened. He saw Dusty come slowly out into the open and, raising his great head, gaze up the valley. For a little time he stood there looking, then suddenly he started with nose to the ground, running rapidly in this direction. Matt grinned with great satisfaction. He leaped on his horse and rode up the river. He must not be caught here. How far would Dusty follow? That was what Matt wondered.

A mile up the river from this point, a narrow sandy stream known as Stranger Creek emptied into the river. Matt quickly rode up to this creek and, turning to the right, passed

quickly through the shady woods toward the
open plain not far away. At the edge of the
woods here he tied his horse, ran back a little
way on his own trail and hid near the creek
bank and waited. In due time he was again
thrilled by seeing the big form of Dusty coming up the creek. Matt saw him walk down
the sandy margin of the stream and lap the
water. Then he saw him turn and begin to
smell Matt's trail. He had just started up toward the place where Matt was hidden when
a thing happened that startled Matt violently. All at once there appeared from the
other side of the shallow creek a huge black
form, and in an instant the black wolf, seeing Dusty, rushed across the shallow creek
toward him. Dusty was so startled he stopped
with a jerk and whirled to run directly back
on his own trail, but the stream was so narrow and shallow and the black wolf rushed
so swiftly that Dusty had to defend himself.

Matt saw him in a thrilling pose. He whirled and stopped, his ears laid flat to his head, his long fangs gleaming, and as the black wolf rushed Dusty met him and slashed with the quickness of a rattlesnake. The two were instantly in violent combat. For a second Matt was so astonished he did nothing but look and in that time he saw much. He saw Dusty whirl and guard himself with his great fangs, saw him slashed once, but saw him slash the black wolf savagely in return.

Matt's gun was on the saddle—too far away, he thought. He must help Dusty instantly. He caught up a piece of dead limb and rushed toward the fighters.

Then a strange thing happened in this lonely place of the old West. Matt Henderson actually entered into the midst of a mortal battle between a wild dog and a huge black timber wolf. But Matt gave no thought to this unusual happening. Raised in the wild

himself, he had learned to act first. That's
what he did now. He rushed in with up-
raised club and struck so quickly he brought
it down on the back of the monster black
wolf. It would be impossible to know which
of these three were most startled, Matt,
Dusty or the big timber wolf. But both dog
and wolf, seeing a man upon them, forgot
each other and both acted according to their
nature, and acted instantly. Dusty uttered a
low yelp of fear and ran swiftly back on his
trail, while the black wolf whirled as if to
face Matt but seeing the way clear rushed
back across the shallow creek and disappeared
in the woods on the other side.

Matt ran up the creek to his horse,
mounted and rode out of the creek woods to
the level land. Far down the valley he saw
the big form of Dusty as he galloped in long
billowy strides. Matt rode down the valley at
a slow canter but he knew it was no use to

try to come up to Dusty. He saw him turn toward the line of hills on the north and run up a rocky hillside at an angle until he was just at the top where a mass of great gray rocks hid him completely. Matt rode on across the valley and then, on reaching the foot of the hill, he rode on up, keeping his eyes on the mass of rocks high above. Suddenly he saw, just above the topmost rock, the head of Dusty. Matt could see the big head against the skyline and he saw that Dusty's ears were cocked slightly as he looked down at the lone rider.

Matt was delighted. Dusty was watching him and Matt believed that he was more curious than afraid. Would Dusty try to follow him again? Matt believed he might. Accordingly he rode back and on down the valley, and still on and on, down the river valley until he came to a giant cottonwood tree. He rode behind the big tree, dismounted, held his

horse, and peeped around. For a minute Matt
saw nothing but the thickets and rocks along
the hillside. Then he saw Dusty emerge from
some bushes at the foot of the hill and start
down the valley. He was coming with his
nose to the ground.

Quickly Matt mounted his horse and rode
away. He rode down into a dry gully and on
over this sandy bed until he came to a region
with which he was very familiar. It was a
place of long winding ridges and many dry
coulees, with, here and there, clumps of trees
one could hide behind. Matt chose this way
purposely so that he might look back on his
trail and not be seen.

Three times in this long ride Matt pulled
up his horse where he was hidden and looked
back. Each time, after watching for a little,
he was thrilled at seeing the great dusty form
of the dog coming on, with his nose to the
ground. Now and then Dusty raised his head

to look forward. Matt thought that Dusty might come close to the ranch house if nothing appeared to scare him. With this thought in mind Matt rode swiftly ahead. He reached one of the ranch stables, took his horse inside and tied him. Then Matt quickly got into some woods from where he could see out on the trail over which he had just ridden. He knew there was no one in the ranch house except old Ben, who at this time of mid-afternoon was probably taking a nap. All was still around the place. There was not even a leaf stirring in the trees. The only sound that came to Matt's ears was that made by his horse in the stable as the animal rubbed his neck against a post. Suddenly Matt's eyes opened wide. He saw Dusty come up from a low draw only a little distance away, but quickly he dodged out of sight again in the draw as if he had seen something to frighten him. However, his head appeared above the rim again and he was evidently looking toward the ranch house and the stables.

After a little time Dusty leaped out of the low place and ran like a streak to Cougar Gorge. And Matt saw the white spots on him as he made his way up and along the side of the gorge until he reached a point high up among the ledges. There he saw Dusty stop, look down on the ranch house below, then, as if he had done so many times before, bend down and crawl out of sight into a den up there.

By moving with great caution Matt managed to get into one of the stables unseen. There he peeped through a crack at the den above that was so near the house. For a time he could see nothing but the trees and bare rocks around the den, and then he saw a movement. Looking intently, he saw another movement when Dusty's head, and his head only, was pushed out of a thicket near the den where he lay quietly looking out.

Matt believed he knew the truth—Dusty had hidden here all winter, near the place where he could get food. While Matt stood peeping through the crack in the stable he thought of possible ways to get hold of Dusty. It might be that if he were seen out on the range in the open by a few of the riders, a skilled man with a rope might rope him. Rolland had roped two mountain lions and nothing could be harder to rope than those creatures. But the thought of roping Dusty and the dreadful fright that would come as a result were distasteful to Matt. If caught in this way Dusty would be frightened nearly to death. And wolf traps would not do either. Dusty would fight terribly if caught in one. A leg might be broken. Then a thought came to Matt. Maybe the old horse corral, not used this summer and only a little

distance from the house, might be used. Old
Ben, with his many ideas, would help if he
thought that was the best way.

Matt walked casually from the south side
of the stable and got in the house just as old
Ben got up from his nap. At once Matt told
him everything. Ben sat in a chair with a grin
on his face, his eyes twinkling. He said,
"Son, how'll we get him and not hurt him?"
Matt mentioned the old corral. Ben's eyes
narrowed for a time. Then he said, "I think
we can work it out. Anyway, we'll try.

"I think he'll stay in that den," Ben went
on. "You helped him when he was in a heap
of trouble. The fact that he's made his den
up there has been, I reckon, a good deal on
account he's found he can sneak up at night
and get grub here. But it ain't all that. If it
was, why would he have followed on your
trail today until he found you? No, it was as
much you as anything else that made him

come here and I bet anything if you can get him so he can't get away, and you keep feeding him, and go easy like, why, he'll tame down in no time. Now it's still some time until Rolland and the others come in, and let's go out and fix that old corral. There won't be much to do. We can be ready tonight, but don't be surprised if we have to wait several nights. In time Dusty will go in that corral for the table scraps on account he'll be so hungry and that's the only place they'll be. I think we can catch him and not hurt him a bit. We'll see."

X

The Cunning of Old Ben

TO make a trap of the unused horse corral
was not difficult. A tall post, with a groove
well greased in the top of it, was set in the
center of the corral. A long lariat rope was
then stretched from the open gate across the
groove and allowed to hang down a little
from the post. On the end of the rope, hanging from the groove in the post, a piece of
beef would be tied. Old Ben's plan was simple. If Dusty was hungry enough, and not too
suspicious, he would come into the corral,
stand up and reach the meat with his jaws,

and try to pull it down. This act would quickly pull the gate shut while at the same time a wooden pin would drop in place and lock it.

That same afternoon the post was set and all made ready, except the meat was not fixed to the rope dangling from the post. As Matt and Ben stood in the shadows of the trees beside the old corral, Ben said, "We'll have to move slow, Matt, on account if we try to catch him too quick he may light out for new country, and we better throw his grub outside the corral for a couple of nights so he'll get used to the place."

That evening Matt threw the table scraps in the corral and a few just outside, near the gate. He and old Ben stayed up that night for two hours watching from Matt's room. At last they saw a movement out in the shadows near the trap, and they saw Dusty clearly as he moved over the ground where there were splashes of moonlight. The next morning all the food was gone. This happened the next night also.

Now came the test. Ben tied the piece of meat to the rope dangling from the post and all was ready. Only a small handful of food was thrown loose in the corral.

That night while the time dragged on neither Ben nor Matt saw more than the shadows around the place. At last old Ben went to his bed in another part of the house and fell asleep. Matt, not long after this, became so sleepy he could scarcely keep his eyes open. But he fought against sleep. He had not removed his clothing. Matt moved over and sat in a chair, a little back from the open window in the shadows of the room. The moon shone brightly on this side of the ranch house and a great splash of moonlight lay just outside the window. As Matt sat looking intently toward the corral he thought a number of times he heard some unusual sound, but each time it proved to be only some movement of the horses. The time slipped by. A little breeze sprang up and Matt heard the whispering of the leaves in the trees and the wind blew gently through the window and against his face. Then the wind died away and there was silence again.

Suddenly Matt straightened up with a jerk. He was watching for Dusty out in the yard and expecting to see him some distance away, but without the slightest warning, not even a sound, Dusty padded around the corner of the house and stood in the moonlight not a dozen feet from the open window of the room where Matt sat waiting. Matt's lower jaw dropped unconsciously and he was almost afraid to breathe for fear Dusty would see him and become frightened. Matt knew he was in the shadows and it was not likely Dusty could see him, but certainly he could scent him, and at this moment Dusty stretched his head forward and tilted his nose up slightly as a dog does when he is carefully investigating any particular scent. For a little time Dusty did this, and then to Matt's anxiety he moved slowly toward the open window. He came not more than a few feet, then stopped and again sniffed the air as he had done before.

Suddenly some horses out in a corral by the stable made a sudden commotion by crowding each other and Dusty turned quickly to look in that direction. For a minute he stood sidewise and Matt saw how big he was. While Dusty stood there many thoughts rushed through Matt's mind. If Rolland, the expert with a rope, was only hiding at the corner of the house, how easy it would be to rope this remarkable dog! But alas! There was Dusty, astonishingly near, but as free as the wildest animal on the range.

The truth was that Dusty did scent Matt on this night and he had come even closer to the house than he had ever done before. Matt had a strange drawing power over him. Not that Dusty was not afraid of him. He was afraid and yet he desired more and more to be near Matt while at the same time keeping out of sight. But he saw not the slightest movement in the dark room, for Matt was as still as if he had been a part of the darkness.

Dusty turned and walked toward the corral in the center of which was the harmless-looking post. He stopped once and looked back toward the place where Matt sat in the shadows of the room, then with nose to the ground, he went to the corral and Matt heard him eating the few beef bones that had been thrown in the corral. Having eaten these, Dusty stood in the space made by the open gate, but he stood there only a very brief time. He looked back once more toward the silent house, then walked inside. Matt saw him moving about inside the corral, and saw him, through the open gate, as he walked to the post in the corral. For a little time Matt could see him as he stood in the moonlight looking up toward the top of the post and Matt was sure he was smelling and looking at the meat tied on the rope there. Then Dusty walked around the post and stood in the corral, looking first in one direction, then another.

All was not quite clear in his mind. It seemed to him that there might possibly be a trick here, but it seemed more likely that this piece of meat hanging up on the post there had been placed to keep him or any other animal from taking it away. And it was this last thought that made him act. He looked once more toward the house and then he looked up at the meat and the saliva drooled from his mouth as he smelled the delicious food. Seemingly no one at the house was looking and it was so quiet out here in the night that Dusty decided that he would stand up on his hind legs, get the piece of beef, and carry it away where he could feast unseen. Accordingly, he stood on his hind legs and for a little Matt saw with awe how tall he was. Matt sat with open mouth looking, wondering if the trap would work. He saw Dusty stand for a second, then saw him as he came down with a jerk. He had set his big teeth in the meat and as he came down he put most of his weight on the pull. Then it happened. The meat came down with Dusty and at the same time the silence of the night was shattered by the slam of the gate as it shut, followed instantly by the dull sound of the wooden bar that fell in place outside the gate.

The sound scared Dusty and he left the meat to run for the opening in the corral. To his great fright he found the gate shut. Instantly he forgot the food, and Matt could see him as he stood before the gate and he heard distinctly a low anxious whine. Dusty began to run around the small corral, searching for a place to escape. Then Matt saw him go to the middle of the corral and run for the gate, saw him leap and for a second he seemed almost over.

But he dropped to the ground and trotted back a distance. Matt saw him through the spaces in the corral poles. Dusty stood for a little time looking toward the high gate which was made of boards with narrow open spaces between. Suddenly he rushed toward the gate. Up he went and this time he actually got his forepaws over the gate and began desperately holding on and at the same time clawing and pushing up with his hind feet. Fearful that he might escape, Matt rushed out and ran to the corral while Dusty was struggling to get over. With a yelp of fright Dusty dropped back when he saw Matt running up. Back to the farthest part of the corral Dusty ran, and there he crouched in fear of Matt who stood at the gate looking in at him.

Matt did not know for a minute what to do. At least he had got Dusty, but it seemed he might escape unless he was watched constantly. Rolland slept in a room on this side of the house and he could hear easily. So Matt shouted loudly, "Hey! Rolland, come out here!"

These men of the West were easily awakened, and this loud call of a human voice startled them. Instantly, it seemed to Matt, he heard Rolland's voice at an open window, calling out, "That you, Matt?"

"Yes, I got Dusty out here in the corral. I'm afraid he'll jump out."

Almost in no time, not only Rolland but

old Ben and a dozen riders came out to the corral. Matt told them what had happened.

Rolland said at once, "Several of us will stay here till morning. A feller wouldn't think that big dog could get over this gate but he might."

Accordingly blankets were brought out and six of the men lay down on the ground at various points close to the corral. Rolland sat on the ground in front of the gate, lit his pipe, and said, "Matt, a young feller like you needs sleep. You go to sleep. Me and Charley and the others here will see that Dusty's still in there when daylight comes and then we'll get a collar and chain on him, although I reckon he'll make it lively for us while we're doing it."

Matt lay down not far from the corral and he was so wide awake that it seemed to him he would never be sleepy, but in less than a half hour he went off into a dreamy sleep.

And while he slept he dreamed that Rolland and the other men were all on horses running Dusty and trying to lasso him with their long lariat ropes. Across valleys, up hill and down, Dusty ran, but no matter where he ran nor how fast he ran, the men on the horses were right behind him, and the long, lithe, sun-tanned Rolland Horn was out in front swinging his loop toward the head of Dusty.

XI

In the High Corral

MATT was awakened by Rolland's voice close by, saying, "Wake up, Matt! We are ready with a collar and chain for this wild Dusty dog! Now you better go in the house and look from the window on account Dusty won't like what Charley and Jim and the rest of us will do to him. And if you hide so he can't see you maybe he won't think you had anything to do with taking him like this."

This seemed like good advice to Matt. He hurried in the house and sat in a chair where he could look out at the horse corral. Rolland

181

and Charley went into the corral with their ropes. Dusty got back as far as he could against one side of the corral, and as the two walked slowly toward him, he watched them with wild eyes. They got so close to him Dusty thought he could run past them and he tried to, but a loop shot out and all at once he found the thing holding him. He jumped back and fought but Rolland held and Charley tossed his own loop over Dusty's head. He was held so that he could do nothing and he began to feel the ropes tightening. This made him frantic, but as soon as the second loop went over his head other men came quickly into the corral with the collar and chain, and while Dusty tried to fight they worked from behind and quickly buckled the collar around his neck. One of the men stood off some distance holding the end of the chain, and Charley loosened the loops and flipped them from off Dusty's neck. Rolland and Charley stood inside the corral by the gate. Slowly now they opened the gate and slowly Rolland began to pull on the long chain snapped on Dusty's collar. Dusty fought back with all his might but Rolland pulled and half dragged him out of the corral to a nearby cattle shelter. This had a good roof and was closed on three sides, the south side being open. Here Dusty was chained to a post and the men went away.

"Now," said Rolland, "we'll leave him to Matt. I reckon he'll be plumb disgusted with fellers such as us but likely Matt will seem different to him. This shed will give him shelter from the storms and he won't feel quite like he would if we shut him up in a dark stable. I hope he won't just pine away now and die. But Matt will do his best and if we see Dusty's going to lay down and die on account he's so lonesome for the wild places we'll have to turn him loose."

From the window Matt had seen everything. He waited until the sun was well up
and Rolland and the other men had gone out
on the range for the day, then he carried a
bucket of water out and set it just inside the
shed. He also took choice pieces of beef with
the fat on, and these he laid carefully near
the bucket of water. Very wisely then he
walked away, saying nothing at all to Dusty
on this first day. In the meantime Dusty lay
at the end of his chain, far back in one corner
of the shed. If there had been a hole or a den
here he would have gone into it. As it was he
lay there and shivered with fear, knowing he
was at the mercy of all these two-legged
creatures around him. But after Matt had
gone away Dusty raised his head and looked
in the direction he had gone. To Dusty that
two-legged creature was somehow different.
It was he who had brought the water and the
food to the den when things were bad. And

now he had brought food and water again and had gone quietly away. He had not stood and stared at Dusty when he could have done nothing but lie in his corner, afraid at being caught here. The youth had only brought good things and then gone away. He had not been with those who had used the ropes and done all this. His scent was different from all the rest.

After a long time Dusty raised his head and, pointing his nose toward the small grove of trees near the house where Matt had disappeared, he sniffed the air. Matt was far back and well hidden among the trees but he could see Dusty. He saw him as he at last got up, stood on his feet for a time, then walked watchfully forward and began to drink from the full pail of water. Matt knew he must be very thirsty. After the strain he had been through he would want water more than anything. He might not eat for a long time but he must have water to live. A horse was the same way, and man also was the same. Matt knew all this and he stood and watched intently through the thickets while Dusty lapped the water from the bucket as if he would never cease. At length, however, he quit lapping and, licking his lips, he stood looking around him. After a time Matt saw him try to get free. He walked out to the end of his chain, turned and pulled back and fought with all his might to get loose. He made no sound, just fought to pull his head from the collar.

Matt was afraid he might jerk free and he called out from the grove, speaking Dusty's name. At once Dusty quit struggling and darted into his corner and crouched down there. Slowly Matt walked from the grove of trees and slowly he came on toward the shed, talking softly as he came. Dusty lay in the corner and looked at Matt with wild eyes,

eyes with greenish fire in them as in all wild
things at bay. Matt came on slowly and
stopped by the bucket of water. He saw that
most of it was gone. Slowly he stooped down,
picked up the bucket, went to the house to
fill it, then walking very slowly brought it
back and put it down. He sat down near it
and quietly talked to Dusty. But Dusty
crouched in his corner, and Matt saw the
look of terror in his eyes. At last Matt went
away. Toward evening he came again, and
again he talked softly to Dusty.

So it was that the days went by, and as was
agreed, no one came near the shed except
Matt. Each day Matt came out to the place
and put fresh water in the bucket and each
day he saw that much of the water had gone.
Only a little of the beef was gone, but at the
end of a week Dusty was eating more of the
food. And at the end of two weeks he was
eating still more.

Then one morning Matt was highly pleased. The meat was all gone and certainly Dusty had eaten it, for no creature would dare come within reach of that great, wild dog lying there. Matt, on this morning, again put raw beef near him and went away. When he came up that afternoon all the beef was gone. Matt got still more beef and this time he walked to within six feet of Dusty, talking softly to him all the time, and he laid down the piece of beef only a few feet away. Dusty kept to his corner with his head low as usual, but Matt saw that he no longer looked with the fierce eyes of a wild thing. Somehow, to Matt, Dusty looked more like a tame dog in utter misery. There was a tired look in his eyes. Matt sat down on the ground in the shed and talked to Dusty for a long time. Always before, Dusty's eyes were wide open and there was a flash in them that told he was ready for instant action. But it

was not so at this time. He lay with eyes half
closed and he seemed to have given up. Matt
looked toward the ranch house. No one was
in sight. Would it be safe to go nearer to
Dusty? Matt had on strong gloves but no
other protection. He picked up a piece of raw
beef and moved nearer and nearer until he
was within a foot of Dusty's nose. There he
dropped the piece of meat and stood for a
few seconds talking quietly. He then started
slowly backing away, and to his great surprise
when he got back some ten feet Dusty raised
his head, looked at him and uttered a real
dog whine. A little thrill went all through
Matt. To him that was an anxious whine.
And as Dusty looked at him Matt thought he
read all of the dog's feelings. He seemed to
say, "Are you going away again to leave me
here in all this? It's pretty bad here. Night
and day I'm chained like this. My body
aches from this confinement and I'm afraid

for my life here, except for you. I don't understand you but it was you who gave me
water and food when I was near death in the
den and now, here you are again, with the
things I need. I'm a little afraid of you, too,
but I'm lonely when you leave. I wish you
would do something to get me out of all
this."

All this went through Matt's mind. He
believed that was about what Dusty would
have said if he could have talked. And in
after days Matt never had reason to change
his mind about this. He was glad when Dusty
plainly whined to him, telling him he was
miserable tied here and that at last he trusted
Matt, somewhat at least. Matt looked toward
the ranch house. No one was in sight. He
knew this was all the better. Dusty was like
a young coyote that has been raised by a man.
The coyote will even play with this one man
but becomes instantly wild and scared at the

approach of any other man. Matt said aloud, "No, I won't go away just yet, Dusty. I'll stay awhile. How would you like to come up and eat a piece of meat from my hand?" Hereupon Matt cut off a piece of the beef and going close, leaned over and held the meat out to him and said softly, "Come on, Dusty. Eat it. It's good." Matt knew the words did not matter. Any words would do. It was the sound of his voice that counted, and he was surprised and delighted when Dusty raised his head higher, looked eagerly toward the meat and then toward Matt. Matt kept coaxing, and he was thrilled again when Dusty without getting up, reached out his head and neck as far as he could, and Matt, not daring to take another step, leaned over and reached out until Dusty's great red tongue touched his hand once and then the great fangs took the meat and it was gulped down. Again Dusty uttered a whine like the first one Matt had heard. Matt moved slowly, cut off a few pieces of meat and again held a piece to Dusty's mouth, and Dusty took it at once and began a series of queer whines, and his long tail thumped the ground three times.

A minute later Rolland Horn happened to look out toward the shed. He exclaimed to some of the men nearby, "Well, I be daggoned! Look out there! Matt's feeding that big wild Dusty and both of 'em act plumb acquainted!" Exclamations of awe and surprise came from the men when they saw Matt standing close to Dusty, who was standing up now, actually wagging his tail while Matt fed him pieces of meat.

From this day on it was clear that Dusty had given himself wholly to Matt. After Matt had actually touched Dusty and Dusty himself felt this touch, all was well. At the end of another week Matt was able to lead him about with the chain. Rolland and the men were careful, and as Matt led Dusty nearer to them, by common agreement they paid no attention to him. The result was that within a few weeks after Matt had got his hands on Dusty, Rolland and the others could stand close and look while Matt held the chain, but it was noticeable that Dusty was uneasy. At such times he would stand and look straight up into the face of Matt, and no matter how much Rolland and the others talked to him, he had eyes only for Matt. It seemed that he was saying to Matt, "If you think it is safe for them to be so close I'll agree. Whatever you think is best for me, I will do."

But as the days passed Dusty became more and more friendly with the men. By the first of August he was allowed to go free and he would come running to the house at the call of Matt, and soon of the other men. At night he slept just outside the house beneath Matt's window. Matt had tried three times to have Dusty sleep in the room on the floor, but Dusty showed he was so ill at ease each time, by pacing the floor and looking out, that after the third attempt Matt let him out, saying as he rubbed his big side, "Very well, Dusty. I won't shut you up in the house if you want to sleep outside. Now don't run off and leave me. But you would never do that, I know." Dusty did not understand these words but he did understand Matt's hand on him and the friend that patted his sides and said the words.

Some time went by and during the hours of darkness Dusty dozed beneath Matt's window. Then, very late one night, long after Matt had gone to sleep and all the house was still, Dusty felt an unusual restlessness coming over him. He had strange dreams in his sleep and once he dreamed the two black wolves were rushing at him. He awakened quickly; his eyes shone with a wild fire and the hair stood on his great neck. Dusty stood up and looked about him. He was grown now, and a magnificent specimen of a dog he was, weighing fully one hundred and fifty pounds. He stood for a minute with his ears slightly raised, listening to the mysterious sounds of the night. Once he turned, looked toward the window of the room where Matt lay sleeping, and uttered a very low sound which said he wanted to roam far away into the night and he hoped Matt would not care. For a time Dusty stood in doubt as he looked toward Matt's window, but the urge was so strong he started away at a lope, his head up, watching, keenly alert, trying to see any animal that might be abroad in the night.

Since Dusty had been domesticated at the ranch he had never run far away during the night. But now his powerful muscles seemed

to urge him on to an endless run across the
wild range. As he ran on, the daylight came.
It was now time for the cowboys to ride out
on the range. But Dusty did not think of this.
He ran on, at times with his head up and at
times with his nose to the ground. All at once
he stopped. His whole attitude changed. The
hair stood on his neck but he made no sound;
he only stood as still as the thick-set silent
gray rocks around him. Dusty scented the
trail of the black wolf. He was no longer
afraid of this enemy, yet he knew the danger
and he was cautious. He could have gone
back but instead he went slowly forward, as
a cat moves when going toward game. The
trail was fresh. Dusty knew the enemy could
not be far distant. Suddenly he stopped again.
He smelled another wolf track. This was another timber wolf, one of gray color, that had
lately come on the range and frequently
helped the black wolf in running down the

cattle. And while Dusty as yet did not know, both these beasts were at the moment crouching not far beyond on the boulder-studded ground, crouching and watching a heifer that was walking away from a number of grazing cows and toward a spring of water just below a mass of big rocks at the foot of a slope.

Suddenly Dusty crouched to the ground and hid near a boulder. A little breeze had carried the scent of the two wolves to him and he knew by the strong scent that they were only a short distance away.

XII

The Gray Wolf Pack

THE masses of boulders hid both the timber wolves and Dusty from the unsuspecting heifer. She came slowly toward the spring but she neither saw nor smelled the enemy here. As she walked on she looked forward with the wild, dumb look of all range cattle that grow up in danger of wild animals. A short distance away the remainder of the herd went on grazing, their heads all pointed in the same direction. When the heifer was within twenty yards of the spring she stopped and looked with staring eyes directly ahead of her.

When the heifer stopped, the big black timber wolf took it as a signal that she was suspicious and might run. With hardly a sound he shot out from the rocks. The other wolf followed swiftly. With a loud terrified bawl the heifer whirled, and with tail in the air, ran toward the herd of cattle. Like a flash all the herd went thundering down the narrow valley. It happened that at this same instant Rolland Horn rode up on the hilltop. Instantly he dismounted, jerked his rifle from the saddle and crouched in the cover of the many big boulders. Just then things began to happen all at once.

The big wolf reached the heifer, ran alongside and reached for her nose, caught his victim, swung back with all his weight and she went heels over head, and unusual though it was, she was only slightly hurt as she hit the ground hard. In another flash both wolves would have been at her throat, but to their amazement a huge dog struck the biggest wolf so swiftly that he bowled him over. The wolf is as quick as a snake, and swift though Dusty was, the wolf bounded to his feet like rubber and both wolves attacked Dusty.

Rolland instantly recognized Dusty. And for a little time he looked in awe at the terrific battle below. It was plain that Dusty was a mortal enemy to these wolves, particularly to the big black one. Rolland quickly tied the horse to a small tree and went creeping down the hill under cover of the boulders. He got within one hundred yards of the place when he saw Dusty leap back in the shelter of the rocks behind the spring. There the two wolves could attack him only from the front. Rolland raised his rifle time after time to fire, only to be disappointed when Dusty got in the way. Then Rolland saw a remarkable thing. The two wolves rushed at once but the lighter of the two drove in first, and so swift did Dusty's fangs strike that this wolf fell back on three legs—a front one hanging useless.

When this happened Dusty rushed out in the open and attacked the big black wolf. He drove in three times, and three times he leaped back with hardly a scratch. The black wolf whirled and ran hard down the valley with Dusty running so close to the wolf that Rolland did not dare to fire. Dusty and the black wolf both disappeared around a turn in the valley and Rolland saw where the other wolf lay hidden. One shot from his rifle disposed of this beast.

Rolland quickly mounted and rode in the direction Dusty had taken. After some time he saw both Dusty and the wolf far in the distance. Rolland put his field-glasses to his eyes. The wolf was getting away rapidly by running and dodging across the shelter of a brush-covered valley, but Dusty was still on the trail and Rolland saw him disappear out of sight. He was moving toward what was known as the Deep Canyon country, a place far to the west, so wild and broken that ranchmen in this region were compelled, summer and winter, to try schemes to destroy a pack of cattle-killing wolves that roamed this range. There were a dozen in this pack, most of them being of a grayish color. None of these wolves were of great size. The leader was a yellow-colored wolf, bigger than the others, weighing about one hundred pounds. But what these beasts lacked in great size they made up for in ferocity in destroying cattle on the range. This gray wolf pack kept within a certain range in the Deep Canyon country. And in the same way the savage black wolf kept to the Rolland Horn range and never came out to the country of the yellow wolf and his pack. In these days of the old West gray wolves had their own range and they all kept pretty well to their territory, but Dusty knew nothing of this.

After a time Dusty lost the black wolf's trail but he ran on toward the west, moving at a rapid gallop, still searching for the enemy's trail. Suddenly he found himself in a wild region of low narrow valleys and high rocky hills, in the sides of which were innumerable dark, yawning dens, many of which made excellent hiding places for the gray wolves that roamed this range.

As he stood on a high rocky hill, looking down upon a slow winding stream below, Dusty realized that he was very thirsty. At once he ran down the hill and reached the edge of the bank of the stream. He plunged over the low rim of the bank and landed with his great body in the water near the bank. As he stood here he was quite hidden from the valley above, the bank being some four feet above him. Dusty was tired from his long run, and after drinking all the water he wanted, he made himself comfortable by lying down on the sandy margin of the stream, his forefeet resting in the slow-moving water. His long red tongue lolled out as he breathed comfortably, while he looked across the stream.

He was about to leave the place when he heard the loud bawling of cattle in the valley on the opposite side of the stream. There was a rise of ground on that side so that Dusty could not see the bawling cattle, but presently as they came on he saw them, and what he saw behind them startled him. A big, white-and-red-spotted longhorn steer led the the small herd of cattle. The steer charged over the ridge with a dozen longhorns following. The old steer headed for the stream, but all at once he turned and ran along the valley on that side, up the river. These steers were slim long-legged creatures and could run faster than other cattle, but not fast enough to escape the deadly enemies that followed them.

When the herd of longhorns charged over the ridge and up the valley Dusty saw the gray wolf pack, led by the biggest wolf, sweep over the ridge close behind the cattle. And here they demonstrated their wild savage nature. Even as Dusty jumped to his feet he saw the foremost wolf leap for the nose of a steer, catch him fair, and saw the steer plunge in his mad flight. This steer was quickly done for by the wolves in the rear, and again the wolves all raced for the longhorns where already the big wolf had brought down another.

Dusty hesitated a second, but a second only, just long enough for the first shock of surprise to pass. Then he ran swiftly across

the shallow stream and more swiftly still up
the valley behind the cattle-killing wolves.
Dusty was a strange dog. With all his being
he had been devoted to the only mother he
had ever known—an old she-wolf—and the
tragedy when other timber wolves destroyed Old Gray in the Valley of the Little
Cedar was never forgotten. To Dusty the
mere scent of a timber wolf would start all
the fire of battle in him. And what aroused
his spirit more than ever at this time, and all
unknown to him, was that he was a descend-
ant of thousands of generations of dogs that
were the faithful companions of men.

It was with these feelings of the faithful
dog that Dusty acted. Because of the favor-
able wind and all the excitement he was actually able to reach three of the wolves at the
rear. And by a strange circumstance, Jim
Hunter, the cattleman who owned this range,
rode out at this very moment from a cut in

the hills and saw everything. The reason Jim
Hunter did not start firing at the wolves was
because he recognized Dusty.

It happened one day that Jim Hunter and
several of his riders had seen Dusty when
Rolland Horn and Matt Henderson were in
the western part of the range. The men had
looked at Dusty almost in awe, because of his
great size, and Jim Hunter, in particular, had
admired him. Now, as Jim suddenly pulled
up his horse and looked, he saw Dusty rush
upon the three wolves. It was a furious attack in which Dusty was considerably cut,
but he destroyed two of the wolves by the
fury of his attack and the third wolf ran
away. Meanwhile the rest of the wolves had
suddenly gotten the man scent. They whirled
to the west and Jim saw them run from sight
with Dusty rushing hard behind the biggest
wolf. It all happened so swiftly that Jim

Hunter sat with astonishment on his horse and looked as the beasts disappeared.

Jim rode out on the valley and looked at the two dead wolves. "That's two of 'em Dusty's accounted for," Jim said aloud. "And he's after more of 'em. He's awful unsociable to wolves. Now wouldn't I like to own that big dog! But shucks, no matter if he has run a long way from home, he'll go back—back to Matt. He's just so daggone big and strong he's got to run away now and then like the wolves do." Jim Hunter rode in the direction Dusty had taken since that was in the direction of Jim's ranch. As he rode on night came but the stars and a bright silver moon shone on the range. Across a bright moonlit valley Jim Hunter's horse galloped steadily and Jim's eyes looked sharply at every tree and bush, hoping to see the great form of Dusty glide away. But there was no sign of him and Jim saw only

the bushes and rocks and dark silent trees
along the trail.

In the meantime, when all the wolves had
escaped, it suddenly came to Dusty that he
wanted to leave this strange region and go
home—home to Matt. And with a sure instinct he turned in the right direction. All
else was crowded out of his mind now. Although he had many cuts from his battle
with the wolves, he paid no heed but started
back toward the east at a steady tireless lope,
and as he ran on he became more and more
eager to get away from these strange sur-
roundings.

It was late in the night when Dusty
reached the ranch house. He whined until
he awakened Matt. Matt got up and let him
in the room, and by the light of a lamp he
saw Dusty had a number of bleeding cuts on
him. "Wolves!" said Matt, and when the

other riders got up at daylight and looked, they agreed.

Matt was exceedingly glad Dusty had returned, but he was concerned as to whether Dusty would run away again. Rolland said, "Matt, you better keep him shut in the stable in the daytime after this and in your room at night. It's awful dangerous for him to be out on the range alone."

Matt agreed. It seemed too bad to shut him up day and night but Rolland and the others thought that after a few weeks of this Dusty might stop running away from Matt when on the range.

Three days later Rolland had the good fortune to meet Jim Hunter on the west side of the range and Jim told him what he had seen. That night Rolland told Matt about what Jim had seen. He said, "All the more reason, Matt, why you should keep Dusty at home."

XIII

The Trap near the River

THE mild days of September had passed and deepened into late October when Matt awakened one morning to find the men had all gone—all except old Ben, who was rattling his pots and pans in the kitchen while mumbling to himself and asking when Matt would awaken. Matt wondered why Rolland had not called him, but soon he knew. The day before had been one of unusually hard riding for Matt, and as he was the youngest of the riders by ten years, Rolland and the others had wanted to help him. Often Rolland had said to Matt, "Son, don't try to accomplish all us older fellers do. You are young and must wait for more experience. Things will come all right but it will take time."

All at once Matt thought of something. He got up and dressed hastily, and going to the kitchen he greeted old Ben and took some biscuits for himself and some pieces of meat to feed Dusty. Matt did not even think to tell old Ben about his plans because he was thinking so much about how to carry them out. He knew he would have the whole day to himself and now he could make the old log bear trap that was near the river into a wolf trap. He might catch the black wolf.

When Matt went outside to the stable Dusty greeted him joyously and leaped up to tell him how glad he was. But Matt was in a hurry. He quickly patted Dusty a little, called him a fine dog, gave him his meat and said, "Dusty, I'll have to keep you shut in the stable today." And Matt gave him more meat as he talked to him and patted his great shoulder. Dusty understood not a word, although Matt told him that something must be done to get the black wolf that was killing so many cattle. And when Dusty whined to get out, Matt said, "I know you hate to be shut up like this, but timber wolves are bad company and none of us want you to be with 'em—not any more. So good-by, Dusty, and I'll see you tonight."

Dusty seemed to understand that he was to remain a prisoner. When Matt moved toward the door Dusty stopped whining and lay down on the earthen floor of the stall, but again he uttered a whine, while thumping his tail on the ground as he looked up at Matt. Matt patted him once more on the shoulder and told him that there might be a chance to shoot at one or two wolves, but that if Dusty strayed off and got near them there would be no chance, for fear of hurting him.

Matt was careful to close the door securely at this time. He saddled his horse and the animal stood tied to a post in the yard. Matt's equipment on this morning was his rifle in a leather holster on the saddle, an ax, a hammer, some wire staples, and a roll of new barbed wire that had just come into use at this time, wrapped in heavy canvas so that the sharp barbs would not stick the horse. Matt mounted, then remembered that he had not told anyone, not even old Ben, where he was going. He rode near the house and shouted for old Ben who was half deaf. But old Ben seemed to be outside somewhere. Matt rode away, saying to himself, "It won't matter. I'll be back by sundown, anyway." He rode almost straight north, for it was in that direction many miles away that the log hut stood not far from the river.

Matt believed he could change the log bear trap. He reasoned he could fix the barbed wire around the lower part of the hut where the rotting logs had left an opening. He could roll rocks inside the hut and up to the walls, and if a wolf were caught it would take days for him to escape by digging. Matt thought he might visit the place often so that a wolf, once caught, could not escape. At least, he believed, this fixing up of the old bear trap would be a new way to try to catch wolves and he supposed no harm would come of the scheme even though he failed to trap any of the marauders of the range.

When he got to the hut Matt worked for an hour on the door of the hut and the arrangement to cause it to fly shut when pulled from the inside. After that he went outside and began to cut a sapling to use as a pry to get one of the large logs of the hut back in place. Matt cut three saplings before he was satisfied, and having cut the last one much larger than the others, he hastily trimmed the end of the small tree like a wedge, so that it could be easily used as a lever. Having done this he carelessly dropped the log to one side where it fell among some nearby bushes. Matt thought nothing of this; he simply wanted to get it out of his way for the present.

Even though it was late fall the weather was unusually warm for this time of year, and to Matt it seemed very quiet around him as he worked in this lonely place. As he moved about in his work he stopped now and then to look at his horse, tied in the shallow ravine just below the hut. The horse stood quietly looking toward the nearby river with its long white sandbars and the many clear shallow streams murmuring along over the sand beds. Matt looked for a minute out on the shallow water where some killdeers, although it was late in the season, were running about and calling to one another across the bars. Turning to his work Matt looked closely about him. He saw the coil of glistening barbed wire lying where he had tossed it. The string, holding the coil together, had broken when the coil was dropped to the ground and the strands of wire lay separated somewhat, but it had not tangled much and Matt let it stay there until he was ready to use it. He worked for some time getting rocks inside the hut and along the walls. Well along in the afternoon he was more and more satisfied with his work. He had it in pretty good shape, he believed.

There was still one thing more he thought he would do. Near the bottom, on this side where he worked, one end of a log had fallen down and rested on the ground. There was thus an opening more than a foot wide at this corner. Likely it would have made no differ-

ence, but Matt wanted to fix the old log trap
as it had been when first made. He paused
to rest for a minute, looked back at the long
pole some twelve feet long that he had cut
and let fall in the bushes. He thought he
would use the pry in getting the big log up
in place. He walked over to the long sharpened pole, picked up one end of it and stood
looking at the large opening in the hut. It
came to him that he could close this opening
as well as some others in the hut with the
barbed wire. That would be lighter work
and he was now tired, anyway. He let the
pole fall back in the brush and walked up to
the hut where he sat down to rest in the
clearing.

The day was so warm that he felt inclined
to lie down, but for a minute he sat looking
about him. He saw his horse standing in the
low ravine, looking up at him and moving his
ears back and forth a little. Matt turned his

eyes toward the opening made by the fallen
log and he thought that after he rested a
little it would take only a short time to staple
the wire across the opening. And he felt
more and more like resting. He lay down on
his back and stretched out his long legs. His
left foot encountered the lower heavy log of
the hut where it leaned close to the ground
and Matt idly moved both feet a little to the
right where the opening was wider. At first
it was very comfortable here as he lay at full
length resting. Once he heard his horse blow
through its nose, but the horse was securely
tied in the ravine and Matt felt comfortable.
He was pleasantly conscious that his work
was nearly done, his horse was near at hand
and ready anytime. Pretty soon, Matt
thought, he would get up, staple the barbed
wire over the openings, then ride across the
range where he would find a number of the
cowboys and he would ride home with them.

When Matt had first stretched out to rest every part of him felt comfortable. After a time a small stick, at first not noticed, began to press against him a little but not enough to cause him to change his position. Lazily Matt pondered whether he should get up and finish his work or turn on his side and rest for a while longer. Being youthful he stayed where he was, thinking to himself that after a little time he would get up.

As Matt lay on his back he wondered about Dusty. Of course he was greatly disappointed at being held a prisoner at the ranch house. Dusty was a strange dog to Matt, but Matt had explained him one day by saying, "As a pup he in some way got with the wolves, and somehow Old Gray had raised him." With his mind on Dusty, Matt thought to himself that if the gray wolves on the range were destroyed Dusty likely would stop running away.

At this juncture Matt thought he heard the faint, far distant bawl of a cow. He was not sure because it was so faint, but it reminded him of Rolland and the other men. They were probably miles west of here at the time.

For a few more luxurious minutes Matt lay still. During this time there was not a sound to be heard, not even the slightest breeze stirred. The silence was so profound that it seemed to give out indefinite sounds to Matt's ears, as was always the case in perfect stillness.

XIV

A Prisoner in the Stable

IN the meantime Dusty lay on some hay on the floor of the stall and did nothing but feel his keen disappointment at being left in such a place for the day. Always before, when Matt had left him like this, Dusty had thought of doing nothing but wait miserably through the hours until the time should come when Matt would open the stable door.

But for some reason things were different with Dusty this time. He lay down on the dirt floor for only a few minutes, then got up and began to look about in every part of the

stable he could get his nose into. All the stalls
in the place were empty except one where
an old horse stood dozing, recovering from a
sickness. When Dusty saw the old horse he
looked at him once, then forgot him and all
else except Matt. Somehow on this day it was
worse than ever to be shut in here in the
semi-darkness. Dusty sniffed all around the
log walls of the barn and he did something
he had not done before. At some points on the
dirt floor near the bottom of the log walls he
pawed away a little of the dirt and hay that
lay there. He seemed only experimenting at
first and for some time he moved about, here
and there, pawing so little that it seemed he
was only thinking how impossible it would be
for him actually to dig clear out. Certainly it
would be a tremendous task for him to make
an opening big enough for his great body.
Moreover, the dirt floor was exceedingly
hard.

Presently Dusty went back into a stall and lay down, but he could not remain still and soon got up to smell along the base of the stable walls. He had moved about in this restless way for a while when he stopped at the stable door where there was a crack an inch wide. For a time he stood there and looked intently toward the kitchen door. Twice he saw old Ben come out and throw water out of a pan, then turn and disappear in the house. Dusty did not bark as he had done on similar occasions. He had learned that it did no good, and anyway his mind was different now. A scheme had at last formed in his brain and he did not want old Ben even to think of him. What he wanted was to be alone for a time. He felt a little guilty because others probably would object, yet he felt justified in what he would undertake to do. Matt had done this miserable thing to him—but no matter. No matter what Matt said or did

Dusty simply must get out of here and run across the range until he found him. He would be embarrassed when he came up to Matt but that would be better than staying here in this miserable place.

After watching the kitchen door for a minute and seeing that old Ben showed no signs of coming out, Dusty went quickly to the side of the stable farthest from the kitchen, and there he fell to digging furiously. The upper crust of the dirt floor was so hard he could not scratch it loose, but he fell to it with his great jaws and fangs and tore away the upper crust, spitting out the dirt as best he could. Once he was below the hard surface he made the dirt fly behind him. He dug rapidly for some time and then, panting from his exertion, he leaped over to the stable door and again looked through the crack toward the kitchen door. There was still no sign of old Ben there.

Again Dusty fell to digging harder than ever. In his efforts some of the dirt flew past the several stalls and struck the old horse who aroused from his slumbers with a snort. Dusty stopped quickly. He wanted no noise out here. He again went to the crack in the stable door and looked. He was pleased to see nothing but the silent house.

Again he began digging, and having got down to some loose sandy soil, he sent a rain of earth and gravel behind him. At last, after all this furious digging, he had a large hole under the stable, one big enough for him to crawl through. He squeezed out and stood outside for a minute, panting, his long red tongue hanging out, dotted with bits of straw and dirt. But he waited only a minute to rest, then he trotted to the corner of the stable and peeped around toward the back door of the house. He knew that what he was doing here would be objected to by anyone who saw him,

but if he could slip away unseen there would
be nobody to object! In that brief look Dusty
saw nothing but the closed back door, and
since the stable would make a good screen,
he used it. He ran back of the stable and on
into a timbered gorge not far away, where he
knew he would be entirely out of sight. He
kept under cover until a mile away, then he
ran out on the open land, his nose to the
ground, hunting the trail of Matt's favorite
horse. This was an animal none too trust-
worthy, but Matt liked him very much because of the horse's great endurance.

To Dusty's surprise and delight he found
the trail of this horse within a mile after
leaving the gorge, and with a litle yelp of
gladness, he ran off with his nose to the
ground, streaking across the range, dipping
down into the draws, up and over the ridges,
following the way Matt had guided his horse
some time before. Dusty was not a trail

hound. In hunting he was the kind that de-
pended much on sight, but his nose was good
enough when it came to trailing Matt in this
way.

Mile after mile Dusty ran on the trail of
Matt's horse, seeing little signs of life except
when a bird flew up from the grass or a cot-
tontail rabbit went scurrying for shelter. But
he paid no more attention to these things than
if they had not been. Once he came suddenly
upon a bunch of cattle feeding in a low narrow valley. The cattle jerked up their heads
from grazing and, badly frightened at the
big wolfhound, started running with tails in
the air. But Dusty scarcely looked at them.
His whole being was centered on the trail under his nose. Now and then he uttered low
whines because he wanted so much to find
Matt quickly.

Dusty ran across a level stretch of ground
and reached a small woods near which Matt's
trail led. But here he got another scent—a

fresh one that caused him to dash into the woods and hide. He peeped out at a lone rider galloping across the range and when the rider was out of sight Dusty came out and again ran along on Matt's trail.

He was making good progress over the wild range when he reached a point on the level highland not far from the rim of a shale-covered hill. Suddenly he saw the black wolf moving in a crouching manner toward the rim of the hill. A light breeze was blowing from the wolf toward Dusty, and he was not suspected as he lay in some bunch grass and watched with muscles tense. The big wolf was crouching and moving slowly along because he had got the scent of Matt's horse tied in the ravine at the foot of the steep shale hill.

The wolf had scented the horse and Matt also. But as yet Dusty had not got the scent from where he lay. He saw only the wolf move near the barren shale that lay on the top of the slope. Then Dusty saw him move out of sight just over the hill, but he was close—the scent was strong. This was Dusty's chance! He ran swiftly from his hiding place. The wolf was so intent on what he saw below, and Dusty got so close and rushed so swiftly, that he plunged over the rim of the hill and against the big wolf before the beast could turn. Dusty sank his teeth in the wolf's flank but his rush and his weight sent both of them tumbling down the steep shale hill. Dusty tried to keep his hold but it was broken as he and the wolf tumbled over and over down the steep hill and into the ravine at a point not far from Matt's horse. The wolf leaped to his feet instantly and ran away, but Dusty did not pursue him, for he saw, to his amazement, not only Matt's horse but Matt himself at the log hut a little above! Dusty did not know that Matt, up to this instant, had been asleep.

XV
Dusty and Matt Henderson

WHILE Matt lay idly resting by the hut he became drowsy and in the unusually warm day he went sound asleep. He had actually slept not more than twenty minutes when one of those strange and dangerous tricks of the weather struck the range country. It often happened that in late fall a storm that was bitter cold might strike suddenly. While Matt lay asleep in the warm stillness there came a blast of cold wind from the north that made a low roaring sound in the trees of the ravine. The trees and some nearby bushes broke the wind from Matt, yet he stirred uneasily in his sleep. An experienced man, riding on a wild range in the West and feeling the sudden blast from the north, would have thought at once of shelter since he would have known the danger of these storms.

It is probable that in another minute the change in the weather alone would have awakened Matt, but as it was something else happened that not only awakened him but caused him to act even before he was fully awake. In his drowsy state, half waking, half asleep, he heard the violent snort of his horse; and being a youth of the old West, there shot through his brain the danger to him if he lost his horse on the open range, and this shock aroused him instantly. It all happened at once. Matt turned and to his astonishment saw Dusty and the wolf—the latter running away.

Matt had not the least thought of the log hut or what the position of his legs and feet were in. As it was, his left foot suddenly struck the log, and to his amazement he felt a crushing weight on his right ankle. The shock brought him up sitting. At the same time he made the pain worse by trying to jerk his foot free, because this twisted his ankle.

The big log, held up at one corner by the rotting wood, had broken when Matt's foot struck it as he turned over. The heavy logs of the cabin were mainly cottonwood, these being the trees nearest the place.

When Dusty recovered from his surprise he looked steadily at Matt, and with ears laid back close to his head, his large mouth open and smiling, he ran up to the level above the ravine and there he dropped down on the ground, turned his head and looked out of the corner of his eyes at Matt, while thumping his tail on the ground. He supposed he would be scolded but he would rather be punished than keep away from Matt. Matt called and Dusty ran up, instantly overjoyed, and he began to whine and lick Matt on the cheek.

The thing had been so unforeseen and had happened so quickly that at first it seemed impossible for Matt to realize that he was not only helpless and in pain but that because the cold was increasing he would certainly die here unless help came from some quarter. His leg would have been broken except for a small cavity under the log where a stone had been removed by Matt in his work. In this way most of the weight of the log was kept off Matt's ankle but it pressed down hard enough to hold his foot helpless, as surely as if it were caught in a trap.

At first Matt had been so astonished he did not try hard to get free, but now when he tried to pull his foot out he found it impossible. He sat up, and bending forward, tried to roll the big log over. He pushed with all his might but the end nearest his foot was caught against the end log. He could actually move the big log a little and he pushed and struggled until he was trembling from the strain and beads of sweat stood out on his forehead and rolled down his face. His breath came hard and trembling. He paused to try to catch his breath. Matt for a time was hardly aware that a cold wind was driving down from the north. He merely sat on the ground breathing hard and waiting.

A coyote, loping along the river, suddenly stopped and looked while the biting wind blew his bushy tail aside and stirred the hair on his body. He looked at Matt only a moment, then ran on, looking for shelter from the coming storm. A lone steer that had escaped the fall roundup trotted by on the other side of the ravine. He stopped, and for an instant stared dumbly at the scene, then trotted away swiftly.

Matt thought of digging his foot out but he did not have even a jack knife at hand and there was nothing in reach but a long dead stick, too rotten for the purpose. Suddenly Matt thought Dusty might help. He would bring sticks and stones to Matt as the two always had enjoyed this. Matt looked at the long heavy ten-foot post, sharpened like a wedge at the small end that lay near in the bushes. He doubted if he could make Dusty understand something wholly new. But he would try. Matt lay at full length and picked up a dead stick. He could just touch the post with the end of the stick. He tapped the post with the stick and said, "Bring it here, Dusty! Bring it here!" Dusty jumped to the tapping stick, smelled it, licked it, then came back uncertain, whining. Matt wanted something, Dusty knew. But—*what was it?*

Three times Matt tapped the heavy post and three times Dusty did the same thing. The last time Dusty licked Matt on the cheek, whined miserably and tried to tell Matt how much he wanted to do what was wanted, yet did not know what it was.

Matt was aware of the steadily increasing cold and he was desperate. He knew Dusty had always retrieved anything like a hat or a stick or a stone. Matt tossed a little stone a few feet away and said, "Bring it here, Dusty." Instantly Dusty leaped out and brought the stone, dropping it close to Matt, and whined again, hoping he had done all that was wanted. Matt tossed a little stick and asked Dusty to bring it up, which he did. Then desperately Matt stretched out and tapped the end of the post again with the stick and said, "Bring it here, Dusty, bring it here." Dusty leaped to the end of the post, licked it once and then all of a sudden he understood. He seized the post at the wedge-shaped end and jerked. His teeth slipped off. "Bring it here," Matt said again. Twice Dusty tried the same way and then he set his great fangs farther down in the post and jerked sidewise. The thing was caught at the other end in the mass of brush. The post had been hastily trimmed of its limbs so that many sharp stubs were left protruding. Dusty seized the end where the stubs were and he fought and yanked hard trying to get the thing to Matt.

In his efforts to get the post out of the brush Dusty was so intent that he no longer looked at Matt. He knew now what was wanted. He would jerk with all his might and so move the post a little, then stop and pant, his long tongue lolling out, then with intense determination showing in his eyes he would pull in his tongue, grab the post with his fangs and yank again. Suddenly Dusty

walked along the length of the post, touch-
ing his tongue to it a few times in his anxiety,
hardly knowing what he did; on reaching a
point near the end of the post where it was
caught in the brush, he tried to set his teeth
there. Three times he opened his great jaws
wide but the post kept slipping from him.
The next time his fangs held and slowly he
lifted the heavy thing up a little, and up a
little more, until he had lifted it as high as
he could; then with the heavy end in his
mighty jaws he started slowly backing away.
The post slowly moved with him, bending
the tops of the brush under it until, at last,
Dusty got it out of the brush and halfway to
Matt. He let the post drop while he lay down
panting for breath.

Matt now was chilled with the cold. He
moved a little as best he could and waited.
He saw blood dropping from Dusty's mouth
where the sharp stubs of limbs on the post

had gouged him. Only a few seconds Dusty lay panting for breath. He got up and with a desperate, determined look in his eyes he set his teeth in the post, slowly lifted it up and slowly backed toward Matt.

Matt lay his full length, his fingers moving as though he were trying to reach the post and help. Nearer, and nearer still, Dusty backed toward Matt, and again the strain of the heavy thing was too much for flesh and blood, and Dusty dropped the post and fell down on the ground to get his breath. He was so close Matt could see the violent beats of his heart against his side. But Dusty did not look at Matt. Again, with a low groan, he set his teeth in the post, the stubs again cutting his mouth, and again he began to back toward Matt. Then as Dusty pulled at the post he was in danger so quickly nothing could be done. In his efforts he had swerved a little to one side and as he did so, he stepped into the coil of barbed wire. His front leg plunged into the treacherous barbed coil up to his chest. Instantly a sharp barb pricked his leg and instinctively he tried to jerk his leg free. But he only jerked the sharp barb deeper into his leg. He dropped the end of the post, whined low with the pain and tried again to jerk the leg out.

A coil of this wire was treacherous to an animal and a dog might be helpless if caught in these coiled barbs. Dusty stopped, let his long red tongue hang while he panted, and now looked once at Matt. Matt could see where the barb had stuck and he knew Dusty could not free himself unless he tore his leg badly. Matt did not speak. He waited tensely and forgot his own pain. Dusty stood a few seconds, but no longer. Looking again quickly at Matt he then looked blankly at the ground before him. Dusty was not aware of the ground nor of anything in the world except that he knew that something was the matter with Matt and Matt wanted that post. He felt the shooting pain in his leg where the barbed wire bit in and he felt the stings on the other side of his leg where a coil of the wire lay high up on his leg.

Suddenly Dusty stopped panting and closed his mouth. Matt saw him lunge back with all his might and saw him jerk the leg free from the barbs, and as they cut through the flesh Matt saw the blood streaming from the leg. Instantly Dusty seized the post again and back he lunged with it until Matt got his hands on it. At once Matt sat up and jammed the sharp end of the post under the big log; then with a small stone for a fulcrum, he lifted the log up enough so that his foot was easily dragged free.

Dusty stood close to Matt, licked him on the cheek and uttered low whines, but not because of the pain in his ugly wounds. Matt,

with no word, quickly untied the red handkerchief from his neck and bound it as tight
as he dared around Dusty's streaming wound.
Shortly the blood began to ooze through the
thick bandage. Matt then gripped the wound
hard to stop the bleeding. His hands were
blue from the cold but he did not now feel
the cold. And as he sat on the ground and
gripped the blood-soaked bandage with trembling hand, his face pale, everything fine in a
youth went into the grip on the blood-soaked
handkerchief. Matt gripped the wound until
the blood stopped flowing, then knowing the
bandage would not stay when Dusty traveled,
he took it off.

Matt mounted his horse and started at a
gallop toward the south, with Dusty following. It was already freezing cold and steadily
getting colder, but it was still clear. Surely, it
seemed, the clouds would soon fill all the sky
and the dangerous sleet and snow would

come. But when night fell the sky was still clear and only the cold wind rushed and howled across the hills and lowlands as Matt and Dusty hurried on. As the cold increased in intensity Matt dismounted at times to stamp his feet on the ground to keep them from freezing.

Dusty ran alongside the horse, and never for a moment did he slacken his pace as he ran through the freezing night. The blasts of cold wind struck him and stung his open wounds. He would have liked to stop and ease the pain by licking his cuts but Matt was rushing on and that was all that mattered. As Dusty ran he had the added misery of weakness due to loss of blood, but at last the freezing cold stopped the bleeding of his wounds.

They passed clumps of trees here and there on the valley, and at times the yawning mouth of a ravine opened from a hill and seemed to invite them in. But the only hope was to reach the ranch house before the blizzard struck. On and on Matt urged the horse directly south across the wild range country, Dusty running close alongside. As the horse galloped on Matt saw dark clouds were floating over the face of the sky and as they increased the night quickly grew darker. Presently a fine grain of sleet struck Matt in the face and he urged his horse faster. Only a few stars shone between the scudding clouds and presently clouds filled all the sky as Matt galloped through the cold black night. He felt he must be nearing the ranch, and a minute later he saw a faint light shining down the valley.

The sleet was peppering down harder and Matt urged the horse faster. Just as they were passing a clump of trees, the horse, already nervous, seemed suddenly frightened at something. He leaped violently to one side, plunging in among the trees. The animal leaped so quickly among the trees that Matt had no warning and a limb knocked him from the horse. The horse instantly ran away toward the light shining from the ranch house. And in due time he ran into the shelter of one of the stables.

For a moment Matt lay on the ground, stunned, while Dusty licked his face, whining and trying to tell him this was a bad turn of things, but that Matt must get up and hurry on. Dusty's tongue on Matt's cheeks and the whines in his ears brought him to his senses. He got up and on his numbed feet stumbled along in the night toward the faint light. They had just reached the corner of the house, when all of a sudden a roaring blizzard with sleet and snow drove down upon them. Nearly blinded and gasping, they stumbled in at the ranch house door. Rolland Horn and all the men were up waiting, hoping, yet downcast. As one man they sprang to Matt and Dusty when they stumbled in.

Dusty dropped down on the floor, his head up, panting hard, looking casually at the men, while Rolland and the others heard Matt tell in a few words what had happened. But Matt didn't finish. He couldn't. As he sat on the floor he put one hand over his face and his head bowed down. Dusty got up, licked Matt's cheek and uttered low sounds.

The wind outside roared and howled around the log ranch house while the sleet and snow drove down in blasts of savage fury. But there was a tense stillness in the room except the low sounds made by Dusty as he licked Matt's cheek. Matt took his hand from his face. He patted Dusty quietly several times. Then, in the silence, he dried his eyes with the rough palms of his hands.

Rolland Horn said with infinite kindness, "Let's take off your boots, Son." Matt held his bent knee with his hands to assist while Rolland pulled off the heavy cowhide boots.

"Nothing but frost bit toes, I guess," said Matt.

"That's all, Son," said Rolland, examining them carefully.

Matt said, "That's nothing, but I wish Dusty wasn't so bad cut up."

"I know, Son," Rolland replied. "We been noticing his cuts but they'll heal."

Matt was relieved at this, but a look of concern came on his face when he said, "I wish Dusty wouldn't run out on the range any more. Something may happen to him, away out there alone."

Rolland said, "Don't be troubled, Son. When we get that black wolf my guess is Dusty won't run on the range again alone."

XVI

Dusty Finishes the Cattle Killer

FOR a few weeks Dusty stayed close to the ranch house. Then one morning, on a mild autumn day, he followed Matt who rode across the range to the Buffalo Springs region. It was almost dark when Matt rode home—without Dusty. While the men gathered around, Matt pulled the saddle from his horse and said, "Dusty is hunting that black wolf—I saw the wolf's tracks along the sand of the river and as quick as Dusty smelled them he snarled. The hair stood on his neck and he started away on the trail at a run. I called him but he seemed to forget everything but that wolf. It was getting late but I galloped after him until I lost sight of him in the hills near Buffalo Springs."

Rolland said, "Don't be troubled, Son. If Dusty meets up with that black wolf it'll be a fine day for the buzzards on account Dusty will leave 'em plenty wolf meat."

Three days passed with no sign of Dusty, although the men hunted daily for him. It was nearly sunset of the third day. Matt and all the other riders except Rolland stood in the ranch yard looking at a lone rider coming in from the west. Suddenly Matt said, "It's Rolland and that looks like Dusty coming on a good distance behind."

"It's so," said Charley Stone. "But what's Rolland got on the back of his saddle? Looks like a dead calf. But why would Rolland want to bring in a thing like that?"

On came Rolland Horn and well behind, galloping along, was Dusty. When Rolland rode up the riders looked with astonishment. Rolland had the carcass of the black wolf tied behind the saddle. Few riders except Rolland could have "persuaded" a horse to carry such a thing. The horse, tired and sweating, trembled while the cowboys took the huge carcass of the wolf off and let it fall to the ground. Now Dusty came up. He sniffed the wolf casually. Then, with tongue hanging and panting, he went over to Matt.

Rolland said, "Dusty finished the cattle killer. I got to see the end of the battle. Dusty was all over that wolf like a tiger. Dusty's cut some but not bad. And now, Matt, my guess is he is done running wild on the range. He won't go again unless he goes with you and he'll come back when you do."

And time proved that Rolland was right.

Dusty never again went away from the ranch house except when he went with Matt. He got all the exercise he wanted, running along – side Matt's galloping horse as they covered mile after mile of the wild range country. And now at night Dusty would curl up on his bed close beside Matt's bunk and there peacefully drowse and dream until the night had gone and another sunrise had come, when they would again go forth together— always together, in the free, wild days of the West.